BEHIND THEM, THE HEADLIGHTS DIMMED. THE BRASH halogen beams faded until the path was nearly black.

"Battery's dying," Ox said.

"No way," Cade replied.

From where he stood in the lake, Jonathan saw that Cade was right. Something moved over the truck's hood, down its grille to cover the bulbs. It was a sheet of darkness. A shadow with no source, like a piece of night torn from the sky. Like the shadow spirit he'd seen outside his bedroom window.

Reaper, he thought, remembering how the shadow had reminded him of death's theatrical manifestation.

"What the hell is that?" Ox asked.

And then he found out.

WICKED DEAD

CRUSH

BY
STEFAN PETRUCHA
AND THOMAS PENDLETON

HARPER TEEN
AN IMPRINT OF HARPERCOLLINS PUBLISHERS

Grateful acknowledgment is given to Shaun O'Boyle
for the use of the title page image, © Shaun O'Boyle.
More of his evocative photographs can be seen on
www.oboylephoto.com.

HarperTeen is an imprint of
HarperCollins Publishers.

Wicked Dead: Crush
www.harperteen.com

Library of Congress Cataloging-in-Publication Data
Petrucha, Stefan.
  Crush / by Stefan Petrucha and Thomas Pendleton. —
1st HarperTeen paperback ed.
    p.   cm. — (Wicked dead)
  Summary: Social outcast Jonathan's life turns nightmarish
when his high school tormentors are killed, one by one,
and Jonathan spots a shadowy spirit outside his bedroom
window.
  ISBN 978-0-06-113852-2 (pbk.)
  [1. Supernatural—Fiction. 2. High schools—Fiction.
3. Schools—Fiction. 4. Horror stories.] I. Pendleton,
Thomas, date. II. Title.
PZ7.P44727Cr 2008   2007009130
[Fic]—dc22   CIP
                                                 AC

Typography by Christopher Stengel
❖
First Edition

THOMAS PENDLETON DEDICATES THIS
BOOK TO DALLAS MAYR: THE WICKED
JACK K.

STEFAN PETRUCHA DEDICATES THIS
BOOK TO HIS FELLOW ASTHMA
SUFFERERS THE WORLD OVER.

PROLOGUE

Standing alone in the vast kitchen of Lockwood Orphanage, Daphne looked through the tall windows and watched the last light abandon the tree-scarred sky. A lazy wind whistled through the cracked glass, caressing her cheeks. The tall girl sighed with it, wondering why her skin could feel cold, or it seemed that she could breathe. Wasn't all that for the living? Just what on earth, she wondered, were the rules?

Absently she glanced down and saw her reflection in the top of the long steel counter that stood in front of the windows. A sharp but pleasant face greeted her: smooth skin, bright blue eyes, curled auburn hair, her pleasantly sexy bare neck and collarbone peeking out from the unbuttoned collar of her striped men's pajamas. Just for fun, she made her form fade in and out, testing to see if she could find the precise moment between being there and not.

What were the rules? Where were the lines? How much had death changed her, outside and in? She needed so badly to know, if only to shake a growing sense of guilt and dread. The guilt was for the way they'd been treating Anne lately, playing the bone game without her, abandoning her to the Headmistress. The dread was over the possibility that the three of them, Shirley, Mary and Daphne, had driven the dark-haired girl so far away they'd never be able to trust her again.

She tsked. Should a ghost feel guilt? It didn't seem fair. Hadn't she already paid for all her poor choices, whatever they were, with her life, whatever it was? If only she could remember who she'd been—but until the luck of the bones revealed her story, she couldn't begin to guess.

The room was huge. Remove the counters and the vast tables, and a city bus would fit here easily. There were lots of windows, too, above the tiled walls, set in a foot so the extended sill could hold many a pie or piping-hot dish. Far off, next to the thick oak door that led in, a rubber conveyor belt wove along the wall, once used to carry dirty dishes in from the dining room. A few cracked plates even remained for the rats to poke about.

Daphne tried to concentrate, to think of what the kitchen might be like had it still been full of life. If *she* were still alive. She wanted to believe she'd had integrity then, that she'd been smart and fearless, but also kind and loyal. She hadn't been lately, not really, as a ghost. She'd broken her own agreements without blinking, even enjoyed it.

"Oh well," she muttered. "Obey all the rules and you miss all the fun."

"You sound like Anne," Mary said, stepping through the tiled wall near the larder door. She cupped her right hand to her blond curls, idly fingering them as she walked along the floor to stand next to Daphne. "I saw you leave the dorms. Why so early? It's dangerous to wander before the Headmistress is in her room for the night."

"Some things are worth the risk. I needed some time to think," Daphne said.

"And did you?" Mary asked pleasantly.

Daphne hesitated and looked around. "Where are the others?"

Mary shrugged. "Anne's retrieving the Clutch and Shirley's off in the walls somewhere. It's just us, the old guard."

"Well, what I've been thinking is that we really need to make it up to Anne."

Mary's pleasant expression vanished. "We gave her three extra turns. *Three*."

Daphne shook her head. "No, I mean *really* make it up to her. Make her more part of the group."

Mary winced. "Are you sure you're feeling all right?"

Daphne chuckled. "Think about it. It's self-preservation, really. Our secret's only as strong as we are."

Mary shook her head. "The bones are Anne's only chance to escape this purgatory, just as much as they are ours. She would never do anything to jeopardize that."

"Keep pushing her, and she might," Daphne said. She nodded toward a huge cast-iron stove sitting against a faraway wall like the carcass of an ebony bear. Among all the black a large lump of warm and furry brown waddled about, sniffing and clawing at the bits of ancient grease that clung to the filthy burners. Mary raised her nose at the sight.

Daphne smiled. "See that fellow? Give him some food, maybe you can train him to do tricks for you. But make him feel like he's backed into a corner, and he won't think about it; he'll just fight for his life."

As she spoke, the rat stopped scavenging to look at them. The girls stared back, curious.

"Do you suppose it heard us?" Mary wondered.

Daphne shrugged. "Probably worried we're competition for its meal, as if we still eat. That's my point. It doesn't think, it just acts."

When the rodent went back to its work, Mary turned to Daphne. "I agree that Anne and the rat have a great deal in common, but I don't think being falsely kind would change her nature any more than you can give that rat wings and make it fly. She is what she is, we are what we are."

Daphne made a face. "I, for one, like to think I can always be better."

Mary was about to respond when a metal cabinet door near their feet burst open. Both the rat and the two girls froze as they watched a series of colanders, pots, and pans tumble out and then scatter on the floor. Amidst the mess sat wide-eyed Shirley, chuckling as she looked at her companions through giddy, half-crazed eyes. "I love this place! Who said being stuck in a kitchen your whole life couldn't be fun?"

Daphne leaned toward Mary, so close her lips almost touched her ear. "It's not like the rest of us are such prizes," she whispered. "Shirley's always putting us in danger, but we give *her* our affection."

"That poor girl can't help herself," Mary whispered back.

"And you think Anne can?" Daphne asked, raising an eyebrow.

Mary put her button nose up. "Yes, I suppose deep down that I do. I think Anne chooses to be the way she is. Which is precisely why I find her so intolerable."

Shirley's face twisted briefly into a pout. "What are you two talking about? I'm sorry about the noise, but the whole house seemed so quiet. Dead quiet," she said. At the word "dead" a girlish giggle erupted from her throat.

"It's all right," Daphne said. "But try to be more careful."

"Guess again," a harsh voice said from the doorway. "It's not *all right*. It's not all right at all. You can still hear the freaking echo going down the hallway. Keep that up and you'll bring the Headmistress screaming if she's not on her way already."

Scowling as usual, Anne stepped in. The oak-door entrance was so far off, she was still a good ten yards from the counter. Her long black T-shirt wavered slightly as she strutted along. Daphne realized she was staring at the girl, sizing her up. Glancing to her side, she noticed Mary and Shirley were staring too. They were all still raw from last night, when Anne had foolishly threatened to destroy one of the bones.

After the raven-haired girl covered half the distance between them, she must have noticed their mood, because she slowed and stopped. Anne stiffened and shifted on her hips, actually looking nervous for once. "What? Have I got pieces of the Clutch on my teeth or something?"

"Why? Did you eat it?" Shirley said with a wicked smirk. She rose from the pile of pots on the floor and stood with the others.

Anne belched loudly, put her hand under her T-shirt, and rubbed her tummy as she came nearer. Shirley's smirk erupted into a laugh. Daphne was relieved at the gastric sign of friendliness, even if it was blatantly superficial. At least those two shared a sense of humor.

Any lightness to the mood vanished entirely, though, when Mary asked cattily, "But you *did* bring it, didn't you?"

Clearly annoyed, Anne pulled out the vermilion velvet bag, hooked an index finger beneath the knot in the string, and let it dangle before them. Her stance was defiant, as usual; challenging. It did not set the stage for a quiet evening, and Anne was right about one thing—too much noise was a dangerous thing.

If I'm going to do anything about this, it'd better be right now, Daphne thought, so she pushed Mary slightly behind her as she stepped away from the counter to meet Anne. As she walked, she grinned in as broad and friendly a manner as she was able.

"Anne, it's so good to see you. How are you feeling?" Daphne asked with the deepest possible sincerity.

8

Anne responded with a sour expression. "Oh, someone woke up feeling all Mother Teresa today. Well, save it, Saint Daphne. Nothing's changed, and you're crazy if you think I'm biting that hook."

"That's what *I* said," Mary muttered.

Daphne sighed. "All right, I admit this isn't easy, but I do want to try. I know we haven't always been very supportive of you since your arrival, and it doesn't really matter why. I'd like that to change, starting now. Can't we give it a try?"

Anne pondered the question. "Give me another three turns."

"No!" Mary said, shocked.

Anne snickered. "Then forget it." She walked past Daphne and plopped the bag on the counter. Small, hard things shifted inside it. "I'm not going to pretend we're some lame-ass support group that needs each other's Oprah-love. We're all here for ourselves. We all want one thing—out. I'm just honest enough to admit it."

"Anne, please . . . ," Daphne began.

"Don't bother. I told you it was useless," Mary said. "She is what she is."

"Shove it, Mary," Anne said, circling to the far side of the silvery table. "I'm sick of you. I mean, how long have you been here anyway, like a century? Two? All that time, and have you figured out anything useful about the Headmistress, or the bones, or even what it means to be a ghost? So who's the big loser here? Me or you?"

"That would depend," Mary said stiffly, "entirely on the game you choose to play."

Anne stopped short. Her eyes narrowed, her face changed. Daphne thought she caught a hint of something new there, something wrong. Guilt? Fear? Mary seemed to notice it too, and then Shirley.

And there they all were, just staring at Anne again.

Making the problem worse.

"Whatever," Anne mumbled. "We going to roll the bones, or do the catty thing all night?"

They opened the bag and the small reddish-brown things clattered onto the silvery kitchen table, looking a bit like dinner leftovers—skull, pelvis, thigh, claw, and limb, all from some unknown animal, all picked clean, all carved with different symbols on each side.

"Shirley told the last story, so you're first, Anne," Daphne said.

Maybe if she wins again tonight . . .

Anne looked at the others, grimaced, and scooped up the bones. She concentrated as she shook them in both hands, then rolled them onto the counter. There was no match.

"Doesn't matter," the dark-haired girl said quietly.

"Of course not," Daphne said, trying to sound reassuring. "You'll get another turn."

Anne ignored her. Mary took the bones up next and seemed to take a moment to pray before she let them roll. Whatever deity she was appealing to apparently said no, though, because she lost as well.

Absently, Daphne took them into her hands for her own turn, but her eyes remained on Anne. The dark-haired girl had stepped away from the counter, away from all of them, to lean against a far wall and look around. When Anne noticed Daphne's attention, she glared at her and then went back to scanning the room. She seemed to be checking out all the exits, perhaps imagining in her mind which would be the quickest. But why?

Probably my imagination, Daphne thought. *Why can't we all get past this? It only makes everything ten times as sad, ten times as frightening.*

11

Daphne rolled the bones, sending them to the silvery surface with a small crash. They turned, spun, and settled, but she wasn't looking at the counter—she was still looking at Anne, watching the girl's tense body language, noting the way she kept shifting her sharp shoulders away from the group and putting her eyes squarely to the door.

Where do you get the energy to hate everyone so much?

"Daphne?" Shirley squeaked.

How alone you must feel.

"Daphne?" a softer voice came. Mary's.

Telling everyone and everything to go to hell, Jonathan.

Jonathan?

"Daphne, look at the bones," Mary said.

"Eh?"

She turned and looked down. The three markings matched. She'd won.

And the story, though she barely realized it, had already begun.

Go to hell, Jonathan Barnes thought, looking up at the round, sweaty face of his English teacher. Mr. Weaver hovered over him like an angry bear in a cheap blue sweater-vest, ready to take off his head.

"Answer the question," Weaver said.

This sucked. When the teacher first asked his question, four kids had shot their hands up like Weaver was handing out cash. But did he call on Anni Moss or Derek Peterson or one of the geek twins, Matt and Pat? No. He jabbed his fat finger at Jonathan.

"Mr. Barnes?"

Jonathan shrugged.

"Am I supposed to decipher an answer from that gesture?"

Maybe not, but Jonathan had a gesture the guy could decipher. It consisted of a single finger. Shouldn't take the teacher long to break that code.

"I'll ask you again," Weaver said. "What was Iago's motivation in turning Othello against Desdemona?"

"I guess he didn't like him very much," Jonathan said.

His classmates laughed. Mr. Weaver lowered his head and shook it slowly.

"Well, thank you, Mr. Barnes. I'm sure Shakespeare would appreciate your carefully thought-out response. When jotting down his little play, his greatest concern must have been conveying the notion that Iago didn't like Othello very much. Rarely has a layered piece of classic literature been so brilliantly reduced to the obvious." Weaver gave him a final look of disgust and turned away. "Can anyone else add to what Mr. Barnes has told us, or should we just accept his wisdom and move on?"

The same four hands shot up.

"Yes, Anni?"

Ass, Jonathan thought, bowing his head, pretending to take notes. Of all his teachers, Gary Weaver was the worst. The guy had loathed him on sight and did everything he could to bust Jonathan's chops. Even when Jonathan answered questions correctly, Weaver made a wisecrack, like his hatred was an allergic reaction to Jonathan's presence. He'd been through it before—with teachers, with classmates. After a while, you just got used to the crap and ignored it.

Jonathan looked up from his notes. Scanning the class, his eyes immediately caught sight of a girl in the second row on the far side of the room by the door. His heart raced a little as he gazed at her profile.

Sometimes he thought the only reason he came to class at all was to see Emma O'Neil. She had a beautiful heart-shaped face and short dark hair, almost black, that jutted away from her scalp in a perfectly calculated shrub of spikes. She was a popular girl, but not one of the stuck-up super-model wannabes most of the other privileged girls were. No, Emma was something else. She played piano for the jazz band and worked on the school paper. She didn't seem interested in dance committees or cheerleading. Emma was too cool for that kind of thing, had too much depth. She even said hi to him sometimes. It was always in passing, always too brief, but Jonathan was grateful. It brought some light to the dark. She made school bearable.

"Are you getting this down, Mr. Barnes?" Weaver asked, shocking him out of his thoughts. "It will be on the test."

Jonathan lowered his head and pretended to read over his notes. It wasn't like Jonathan didn't know the answer to Weaver's question. He knew it, but he wasn't going to go through another year as a "brain." That would be like tattooing the word "victim" on his forehead. As it was, he figured he might as well set up appointments for the jocks so none of the "Roid Patrol" missed their chance to throw him against the lockers. Besides, class participation was a minor part of the grading system, and Jonathan always did well on tests. He kept the *A*s to a minimum, for the same reason he didn't volunteer answers in class, but his grade-point average was good enough to get him into a college far away from Westland High School.

On his notepad, he wrote: *Iago was passed over for promotion; Iago was jealous of Othello because he wanted Desdemona for himself.* These were the answers Anni Moss gave, and they seemed to satisfy Mr. Weaver. To these Jonathan added *Iago believed his wife cheated on him by sleeping with Othello (that whole thing about "'twixt my sheets—Has done my office.") And Iago grooves on evil—"If thou canst cuckold him, thou dost thyself a pleasure, me a sport."*

Jonathan appreciated that last line. He'd underlined it in his text, memorized it. It was kind of cold-blooded, but it totally made sense to him: Some people just got off on throwing a hurt. It didn't matter who they were hurting. They just grooved on the humiliation they handed out. The Roid Patrol didn't know him (not really), but that didn't stop them from throwing him up against the lockers every chance they got. It was a sport, a thrill, a quick fix of happy-giggle-fun for a bunch of brain-dead muscle zombies. Same with Mr. Weaver.

Evil tastes like candy, he wrote.

He smiled at this. He cast another quick glance at Emma, then returned his attention to his teacher, who stood at the front of the class holding a tattered old copy of *Othello* in his hand. With the

17

other hand, Weaver yanked down the hem of his blue sweater-vest. The teacher was talking about the result of Iago's deceit, the end of the play.

In his mind, Jonathan pictured Weaver in a long white robe, his sweaty head like a pale pumpkin on top of a draped table. The teacher was stomping back and forth, pointing his finger at Anni Moss, the way he'd used it to pick out Jonathan to answer his question. He imagined Weaver screaming at Anni and lunging forward, grabbing her around the neck and strangling her like Othello did to his wife, Desdemona. Anni's body fell to the linoleum floor, her blond hair fanning out from her lifeless face. Then Weaver pulled out a dagger and said, "I kiss'd thee ere I kill'd thee: no way but this/Killing myself, to die upon a kiss." Then he plunged the knife into his chest. But instead of opening him up and drawing blood, the blade popped the plump teacher like a balloon, causing him to soar around the room making farting noises as he deflated.

Jonathan chuckled at the daydream, looked around to make sure no one was noticing, particularly Emma O'Neil. He'd freak if he saw her looking at him like he was a psych-ward reject.

18

Fortunately, Emma was focused on her notes. But to his surprise and embarrassment, someone else *was* noticing.

She sat three rows ahead of him and to the left, by the window. Her name was Kirsty Sabine, and she was new at Westland High. She was a bland-looking girl with straight dirty-blond hair that fell to her shoulders like a rough cloth. Her face wasn't ugly, but it wasn't pretty, either. It was just plain. Jonathan quickly looked away when he noticed her looking at him. She was even smiling, like they shared the same joke, like she'd seen his thoughts and found the idea of their teacher farting through the room and growing smaller as funny as Jonathan did.

He looked at his notepad, and the first thing he saw was the line *Evil tastes like candy*. He took his pen and scribbled it out.

As expected, he made it halfway to his history class before the Roid Patrol locked their sights on him. He didn't see them coming up from behind, but suddenly he was thrown off balance, his feet lifted off the ground. He hit the wall of lockers hard, causing the dangling combination locks to clatter like applause. His books slid along the floor, and he barely kept his face from joining them. But he'd learned to recover quickly from such attacks. He looked around at the smiling faces passing him in the hall, wondering how many people had seen this latest humiliation (*Not Emma,* he thought. *Please not Emma*). Then he stopped looking, realizing it didn't matter if she was an eyewitness to the event. Everyone in school already knew Jonathan was the Roid Patrol's tackling dummy.

"Nice!" Toby Skabich said with a throaty laugh. He whipped his hand in the air to high-five Merle Atkins (whom everybody called "Ox"). Next to them Cade Cason was doubled over with laughter. They celebrated tossing Jonathan against the lockers as if it were some brilliant football strategy, rather than a daily occurrence that took no more thought or skill than crushing an empty soda can.

Jonathan said nothing. What was the point? He couldn't take them in a fight. No way. Even one on one, he probably couldn't have done much more than land a lucky punch (maybe on Toby . . . no way on Ox or Cade).

Jonathan was built small. Not only was he shorter than most of the other juniors, he was slender. His arms were like twigs, and there didn't seem to be much he could do about it. He'd spent an entire summer going to the YMCA to lift weights, and at home he chugged protein shakes—anything he thought might add some bulk to him—but he was still "Little Jonathan," hardly any different than he'd been in junior high school. His mother told him it was the way God made him and he might as well get used to it. So he avoided confrontations with the Roid Patrol, kept his mouth shut. He might be able to get away with throwing lip at Mr. Weaver (because teachers couldn't really do anything), but the Roid Patrol could hurt him, and they would if he gave them a reason to.

Still laughing and clapping each other on the back, Toby, Ox, and Cade turned into a classroom at the end of the hall. Jonathan knelt down to get his books as other kids pushed past him, eyeing him and smiling, knowing what had occurred whether they had seen it or not.

"Jerks," Jonathan muttered, addressing all of the students, not just the Roid Patrol. Only a handful of kids at Westland High were even remotely cool to him. They nodded to him in the hall, exchanged smart-ass remarks with him in classes. Like the occasional greeting from Emma O'Neil, these interactions were too brief and led to no close friendships. Fact was, he was on his own. He didn't know why. It wasn't like any of the cliques handed out a checklist, telling you why they hated you. His friend David, who unfortunately had been transferred to the "gifted program" at Melling High last year, said it was because Jonathan didn't "try" to fit in. So the kids didn't know what to do with him.

"You're not weird enough to be a geek. Not big enough to be a jock. You're too smart to be a burner. With the way you dress, you'll never join the FBI" (a David-created acronym standing for Fashion Before Intellect). *"You are a unique beast among the herd, and they are bound to see you as a predator or prey."*

Great, Jonathan thought, standing up with his books clutched in his arms. Obviously the herd had decided on prey.

At least his humiliation was complete for the day. The Roid Patrol never struck twice, and his history teacher, Mrs. Locke, was cool—as boring to watch as a snail, but fine. Furthermore, it was Friday. That meant he had two full days to put

Westland High out of his head, before he once again had to step into its dangerous halls.

Of course, that meant two days without seeing Emma O'Neil. That would suck, but at least his shoulder would have a chance to heal.

He couldn't know that certain events would occur over the weekend—events that would change Westland High and his life forever.

Jonathan's home was an apartment in a vast, flat complex north of town. The single-story buildings sat like a hedge maze on a rise above a rocky, nasty field of scrub grass. The white paint on the apartment's walls was graying and glum. It had been that way since his father moved the family in four years ago. It needed a fresh coat of white. But the apartment complex management didn't care, and his father didn't believe in "putting money into other people's property." Truth was, his father didn't believe in putting money much of anywhere that didn't include a betting window or a bar. Jonathan gave up on any hope of an allowance when he was ten years old. Instead, he worked odd jobs in the summers until he turned sixteen; then he filled out an application and was hired by

Bentley Books in the mall, working a couple of nights a week and Saturdays.

The job wasn't going to make him rich or even raise his standard of living. He saved his money for the sole purpose of getting out of town once he graduated from Westland High. Oh, he might crack into his account if Emma agreed to go out on a date with him, but likely that would signal the apocalypse or something. Though his meager savings were not likely to pay for four full years of college, it was a start.

Jonathan walked into the apartment. The lights were off, and he wondered if his father *forgot* to pay the bill again, or if his mother just never got around to turning them on. He tested the light switch. The half-globe fixture in the middle of the living room came on, and he sighed with relief.

In his room he dropped his worn knapsack on the bed and went to his desk. He lifted the phone from its cradle and heard his mother's voice, thin and distorted, skittering over the line. He could tell by how fast she was talking that his aunt, Judy, was on the other end. His mom was always on the phone with her. Every day. Of course, the length of the call depended on how pissed off with his

24

father she was. When William Barnes did some-thing epically stupid—about once a week these days—Jonathan's mother could tie up the phone line for hours, which meant he could forget about checking his email or IM-ing with David.

"Splentastic," he muttered, shaking his head.

Jonathan turned on his computer and waited for the old machine to boot up. The Dell was a hand-me-down. It was his brother Hugh's com-puter, left behind when he took a job on a fishing boat in Alaska with a brand-new Mac laptop he'd won in an internet contest. The Dell wasn't bad, and David had come over one afternoon to install about a thousand bucks' worth of software. It wasn't state of the art, but it would do.

Jonathan was used to making do.

From *The Book of Adrian, Fri. Oct. 7:*
  It's all about fear. Nothing is so frightening as being powerless. In order to feel control, they humiliate and abuse that which they perceive as different. They bolster their own fragile egos, their own worth, by humiliation and attack. It doesn't matter if the target is as small as

an ant, being fried by a magnifying glass, or as fragile as a butterfly whose wings they tear away with the glee of a child opening a gift. *I own this*, they think. *I control this*, and in those moments of petty destruction, they affirm their mastery over something, because deep down, way down where the fear of the dark lives, they know they control nothing.

But I do.

And now, I hold the magnifying glass. I grasp their fragile wings between my fingers.

Isn't that right, Mr. Weaver?

The usual weekend crowd gathered at Bentley Books, wandering through the aisles of new releases and guzzling coffee in the café at the back. Near a cart of books that needed to be shelved in the Self Help section, Jonathan and David stood looking at a hottie in tight jeans bent over to retrieve a diet book from the bottom shelf.

"Explain this to me," David said. "She weighs like five pounds, and she's going to buy a diet book?"

"Skeletal is still the rage."

"Which book do you think she's going to take?"

"I don't know," Jonathan said, closely eyeing the

denim hugging the girl's backside. She shifted her weight in a motion that went straight to Jonathan's head. "But I hope it takes her a long, long time to find it."

David laughed and swatted Jonathan's shoulder. "Amen," he said.

Whereas Jonathan was small of build and thin as a reed, David was a hefty kid with a buzz cut, a round face, wire-framed glasses, and pale blue eyes. They'd been friends for more than three years, and until David's parents had sent him off to Melling, they were nearly inseparable. After Jonathan was hired by Bentley Books, David applied for a position himself, though he certainly didn't need the money. David's dad created software for companies to streamline manufacturing protocols or something like that. David's college tuition was secured long before his birth.

"It's kind of hypnotic," David said, cocking his head to the side as if the motion would give him a new perspective on the girl's backside. "It's like a perfect denim buoy, floating in the ocean, and I must reach out and grab it." To emphasize his point, David extended his hands and clutched at the air like he was testing the firmness of two water balloons. "It's a matter of life and death. It's a hormonal imperative."

"Explain that to the ambulance driver while he's icing down your crotch, because she will knee you so hard you'll know what your children would taste like."

"SAW," David said with a laugh. *SAW* was David-speak for *sick and wrong*.

"We should get back to work," Jonathan said, but made no move to change his position against the cart.

Even when the girl found the book she was looking for and stood up, he kept looking at her. She *was* thin. Probably too thin. But Jonathan had to admit she was the kind of girl he dreamed about. She had the same figure as Emma, and he liked that. Next to a girl like her, he wouldn't look quite as much like a stick figure.

"Come back," David whispered when the girl disappeared behind a row of shelves. "Must . . . touch . . . your . . ."

"Gentlemen?" Both Jonathan and David turned, startled.

Stewart Houseman, the assistant manager, stood beside them. Stewart was a chubby man in his forties with short graying hair and skin the color of cookie dough. The fat in his face weighed down his features, making him look perpetually tired. His eyes were clear though, sharp, and right now they looked amused.

"Hey, Stewart," David said. "We were just taking a little break."

"I know what you were doing," Stewart said. "Just don't be so obvious in the future? We don't want a lawsuit."

Jonathan's face felt red. He looked at his friend, and David was blushing too.

"And," Stewart continued, "if I'm not mistaken, you're supposed to be in General Fiction, aren't you, Jonathan?"

"Yeah," he said. "I was just helping David with the cart."

"Well, he seems to be doing just fine, so why don't you head on over? I'm sure a lot of customers would like your input on which new 'chick-lit' tome they should pick up for the beach."

Yeah. Way funny, Jonathan thought. Stewart was cool enough, for an assistant manager, but his little game of acting all intellectual got really old. Unfortunately, Stewart was the boss, so

Jonathan nodded his head.

"We'll get some liquid speed on break," David said. "See ya."

"Yeah. See ya."

Jonathan was shelving a dozen copies of the new Stephen King paperback when he heard about Mr. Weaver. He was reading a descriptive paragraph on the back cover (even though he had a copy of the book sitting on the floor by his bed at home) when he heard a woman say:

"He taught English at my son's school."

"Oh dear," another woman replied. "The children will be so upset."

"Not if he was anything like my English teacher was."

"That's terrible," the second woman said with a nervous laugh. "Do they know who did it?"

"No, they just found the body this morning."

Jonathan eased closer to the shelves to listen. He could not see the women, but they were directly across from him in the next aisle. Their conversation was as clear as the Muzak on the store's speakers, though far more interesting.

"Xander called me from the police station. He

has the early shift, and he said Weaver was smothered."

Mr. Weaver, Jonathan thought, startled. He
dropped the paperback but quickly snatched it
out of the air before it hit the shelf.

"Smothered? Oh, that's so awful."

"I know. The idea terrifies me. Not being able to
breathe. Xander said it could have taken up to
three minutes before he died. Now, can you just
imagine that? Trying to breathe and struggling and
knowing someone wants to kill you? Three minutes would seem like hours."

"So awful," the second woman repeated. "Who
found him?"

"Well, that's the really weird part. His neighbors
found him . . . because he was in their tree."

"Their tree?"

"That's right. Whoever killed him hauled his
body fifteen feet in the air and threw him over a
branch and left him."

The women walked away, still talking about the
tragic event, leaving Jonathan stunned. He didn't
know how to feel about this news. Sure, Weaver
was an ass, but this was a totally screwed-up situation. Dead? Murdered? Smothered? Draped on a

tree branch like a bit of laundry left to dry? He felt bad for Mr. Weaver. He also felt really weird because he'd never known anyone who'd died before. Even Jonathan's grandparents were still alive, though he rarely got a chance to see them.

Jonathan put the book on the shelf and turned to go find David so he could share the news, but saw Stewart at the end of the aisle. The assistant manager had his arms crossed, nodding his head, chatting with a customer. Stewart threw a glance in Jonathan's direction, letting him know that he was watching and would only take so much dis' before getting all Trump on Jonathan's ass.

Telling David would have to wait until their break. Thirty minutes. It seemed like way too long to hold this information in.

Three minutes would seem like hours.

Jonathan picked up another handful of books and began placing them on the shelf.

"You hated the guy, though. Right?" David asked, clutching his double espresso in his pudgy hand.

"He was crappy to me, but I didn't want him dead."

"Or did you?" David asked, leaning across the

table. His eyes gleamed the way they always did when he was joking around. "I bet you snapped like a glow stick and got all R. Kelly. You decided it was time to teach the word jockey a lesson, so you snuck over to his house and . . . PAC!"

"PAC?"

"Popped a cap," David said, lifting his cup for another sip.

Jonathan laughed, despite finding the whole subject unnerving. "They said he was smothered. Besides, how could I get his body fifteen feet into a tree? He weighed like a thousand pounds."

"Don't mock the girth," David said, patting his belly. "Whoever did it probably hauled him up there with some rope."

"But why do it?" Jonathan wanted to know. "I mean, it's just creep-show stupid."

"Maybe they wanted to play piñata."

"Come on," Jonathan said.

"What? I don't know who'd off him, but my guess is the cops'll have caught the guy before the evening news. I mean, someone had to see something."

"I guess."

Mr. Weaver's death hung over him like a light,

scratchy sheet. He even felt guilty for imagining the guy popping like a balloon, which was stupid, he knew. But he couldn't help feeling it.

He wanted to talk about something else, so he reached across the table and lifted the book David had brought with him on break. Turned out this distraction was little better than what it was meant to distract. The cover was black with red lettering.

History of the Occult, the title read.

"You've got to be kidding."

"It's for a class," David said. "I've got a paper due next week."

"I thought Melling only let you study hard-core brain data."

"Indeed," David said. "My thesis is about how magic was the first science and the first religion. Well, more about being the first science because Melling High fears God talk. But it's like they used magic for medicine, right? So my theory is they approached this from a pseudo-scientific perspective. Trying potions, changing ingredients until they found something that sort of worked. But most early cultures thought sickness had a spiritual cause, right? Possession? Curses? So they

35

added chants and rituals to ward off the evil."

"Move over, Merck pharmaceuticals."

"Don't be laughin' at the mojo," David said. "Some of the stuff I've read is pretty serious. It'll be a cool paper."

"No doubt." Jonathan didn't want to talk about magic any more than he wanted to talk about Mr. Weaver's death. He sat quietly. Drank his coffee.

"Oh," David said, straightening up in his chair, "I think we have a solid eight at one o'clock."

Jonathan turned in his chair and looked across the café to where David indicated. Kirsty Sabine, from his English class, stepped onto the mezzanine where the coffee shop was located. She looked around, cautiously like she expected someone to throw something at her. After scanning the room, she ducked her head and walked to the counter.

"She goes to my school," Jonathan said. "You think she's an eight?"

"What? You don't?"

"Maybe a five."

"No, your mother is a five. *She's* an eight. Besides, what do you care? You already have a fictional relationship with a certain Miss Emma."

36

"Thanks," Jonathan said, embarrassed. "I thought we weren't going to bring that up again."

"Hey, I'm just saying you can't hog all the hotness. The rest of us need imaginary girlfriends too. What's her name?"

"Kirsty."

"Niiice," David said. "Spill. Does she like her men ample or what?"

Jonathan laughed. "Yeah, man. She transferred in at the beginning of the year, and the first thing she said was 'Where are all the chunky guys?'"

"You're just jealous. You know women like a guy with something they can hold on to. They find a little bulk comforting."

"And what twisted talk show told you that?"

"The one in my head," David said. "So, does she have a boyfriend or what?"

"I don't think so. She's always alone at school." *Kind of like me*, Jonathan thought. He looked toward the counter and saw Kirsty paying for her coffee. He tried to see her the way David did, as an eight, but it just wasn't there. Like all girls, he compared her to Emma O'Neil, and to his mind, Kirsty just didn't come close. Maybe no girl could.

"She's making my pants tight," David said.

37

"Thanks for sharing," Jonathan said. "Why don't you go over there and tell her? I'm sure she'd be thrilled to hear it."

"No. I have to play it cool."

"As in . . . watching her until she leaves and never seeing her again?"

"Yes," David said. "Exactly. It's foolproof."

Jonathan couldn't argue against the point. That was basically his tack with Emma. Just sit and watch and dream.

Kirsty carried her coffee to a small table in the back, where Jonathan could see her over David's shoulder. She sat down and immediately opened a book. She lowered her head to read, and her hair fell forward like a curtain to hide her face.

"What's she doing?" David asked. "She's scoping me, right? Looking at the Hulk of Love?"

"She's reading."

"She's way into me," David said, obviously joking. "Hey, we have a new entry into the Dictionary of David. *She's way into me*: SWIM." He laughed. "Yeah, and she's swimmin' with the sharks now, boy."

"Whales maybe."

"Unkind," David said. "Harsh and unkind."

38

"So, what's up for tonight?" Jonathan asked. He was tired of talking about Kirsty Sabine.

"The usual, I guess," David said, draining the last drops of coffee from his cup. "Rent a couple of DVDs, maybe play some PS3."

"Are your parents home?"

"Are my parents *ever* home?"

Monday afternoon Jonathan walked into English class and felt an uncomfortable tug in his chest. A substitute teacher stood at the front of the room, drawing on the blackboard. She was a fine-looking woman, wearing black slacks and a red blouse. But seeing her just made him think about Mr. Weaver. He'd watched the news over the weekend and saw the reports of Mr. Weaver's death, but it didn't seem quite real. Not until now, not until he saw the man's replacement scratching out couplets with colored chalk. He felt awful.

Emma O'Neil was sitting in her chair when Jonathan entered the room. He passed by her, hoping she'd say hi, but her head was down. He could see a sheen of tears on her cheeks. She was mourning for Mr. Weaver, and it made Jonathan feel worse. He crossed the room to his desk near the back, sat down, and rested his chin on his hand.

In his thoughts he didn't go to his chair. No. In his mind, where he could muster bravery, he stopped at Emma's desk and knelt down beside her, put his arm around her shoulders. "It's okay," he said. "Mr. Weaver is in a better place." This made Emma cry, purging the rest of her sadness as she pushed in close to take comfort from Jonathan's embrace. He felt the spiky locks of her hair on his cheek, smelled her perfume, which he imagined smelled like flowers. "I'm here if you need to talk," his brave mind-self whispered.

The daydream warmed him. He wished he could be the person he imagined. Emma looked so miserable, and he wanted to do anything he could to make it stop. She shouldn't be unhappy.

Once the other kids arrived and took their seats, the substitute, Mrs. Taylor, said, "I'm sure you're all very upset about Mr. Weaver's passing, but we'll try to honor his memory by continuing his work."

That's all she said about his dead teacher. It didn't really seem like enough, though Jonathan couldn't say he wanted to hear any more. Checking on Emma, he saw that she was barely keeping it together, and perhaps the less said about Mr. Weaver, the better.

To add to his unease, Kirsty Sabine looked at him during class. Not once. Not twice. But three times Jonathan glanced toward the window and caught the girl looking his way. She was slightly turned in her chair, peering from the corner of her eye. The moment Jonathan noticed her, she looked down or toward the window. Her attention made him uncomfortable, but it wasn't a bad kind of uncomfortable exactly. He may not have thought she was an eight like David did, but a girl was look-ing at him, and she wasn't pointing or laughing. She was just checking him out.

SWIM, Jonathan thought. *Now she's swimmin' with the guppies, boy.*

After class Jonathan stood in the hall by the door, checking up and down the hallway for the Roid Patrol before he attempted to drop off books at his locker. He watched Emma emerge from the class and wander, head down, away from him. His heart ached with each step she took. Classmates filed past him, chatting excitedly about Mr. Weaver or their weekends or both. Finding the coast was clear—no Toby or Cade or Ox in sight—he entered the stream of students moving along the halls. He made it to his locker with no bone-jangling collision and shoved his English text inside. Retrieving his geometry book, he felt an odd tingle rise up on the back of his neck, as if someone were dancing their fingers very near the skin there.

Jonathan closed his locker and was surprised to see Kirsty Sabine. She stood ten lockers down, pushed tight against them as the river of students passed. She looked right at him and, this time, didn't turn away when he noticed.

Instead, she smiled. She lifted her hand in a shy wave.

He nodded his head and quickly looked at the floor, then at his shoes. When he looked up, he turned his head, pretending to watch the herd of students, searching for Kirsty in the corner of his eye.

But she was already gone.

Jonathan scanned the wall where Kirsty had stood but didn't see her. He didn't even catch a glimpse of her in the crowd.

Then Toby Skabich came up from behind and rammed Jonathan with his shoulder. Jonathan lifted off the ground and hit the wall of lockers.

The audience of padlocks applauded.

"Are the Roid Patrol still doing that?" David asked. "I thought they stopped."

"They never stopped," Jonathan replied. He adjusted the phone against his ear. "I just stopped talking about it."

"Well, if it's any consolation, Toby and his boys are going to grow up to be used-car salesmen. Their greatest achievement will likely be beating a series of date-rape charges."

"I'm really getting tired of it."

"I thought your school had a zero-tolerance policy."

"What my school has is a winning football team, the first in like a thousand years. No one is going to do a thing unless there's actual bloodshed. Besides, if I narc them out, they'll just hit me harder."

"I say grab a gun and PAC."

"Knock it off, David. Those guys are graduating

this year. As long as I can make it to June without a concussion, I'll be fine."

"Well," David said. "Someone should do something."

From *The Book of Adrian, Mon. Oct. 10*:

The notion that man has advanced beyond animal instinct is disproved at every turn. It is never more clear than in their cruelty and posturing. Just as a lion will fight to lead his pride, assuring him of the best mate; just as rams will butt heads to win the favor of does; just as a peacock unfurls its tail feathers to attract, men engage in conflict to gain attention and approval of their female counterparts. They fight and preen and pose. It is a fundamental part of the breeding instinct.

In a species set apart by intellect, it seems odd that such base and brutal traits are still coveted or, at the very least, believed to be. Intelligence and imagination should be the aspirations. They should be the peacock's plumage and the lion's might in a species that claims intellectual superiority. Yet they are not. The lions still fight. The rams still butt heads.

Isn't that right, Toby?

After dinner—another gagfest microwave nightmare from the freezer—Jonathan sat in his room,
leaning over the keyboard of his computer, waiting for an MP3 file to download. His computer
only had a dial-up connection, so it took forever.

Mr. Weaver's death was on his mind. He'd seen
the teacher's pudgy face smiling out at him from
the newspaper next to an article that said almost
nothing about the guy's death. He was smothered
and left in a tree. No suspects. No motive. No new
information.

Jonathan's bedroom door cracked open, and his
mother, looking exhausted and really old, poked
her head in. He hadn't seen her since she dropped

the small plastic tray holding his dinner on a plate and handed it across the kitchen counter to him. He'd retreated to his room with the meal.

Now his mother cast an annoyed look at him, as if she'd just caught him tracking mud through the house.

"I need the phone," she said.

"I'll be done in a minute," he said. "I'm downloading a file."

"Well, I need to speak to your aunt."

"Just one more minute."

"Now," she said, sounding really pissed off. "This house doesn't revolve around you, you know?"

"Mom, it's like one more minute."

"Right now!"

The progress bar on his computer still showed a quarter of an inch before the song finished downloading. That could mean another thirty seconds or another three minutes the way his machine worked. It was like in the movies where a guy was waiting for a code, and if he didn't get it in time something would explode.

In this case the something was his mother. He just didn't feel strong enough to deal with it.

"Okay," he said, grabbing his mouse and dragging the cursor over the box to close the connection. He jabbed the mouse button and the window vanished. "I'm done."

His mother threw a final furious look at him. She backed out of the room and slammed the door.

Jonathan hit the desk with his palm, sending a bolt of pain up to his elbow.

Enough of this crap.

He rose from the chair and stomped across the room, threw open the door. In the hallway, he saw his mother's shadow shrinking on the far wall. He charged forward, chasing the ever-smaller stain on the wall, following it into the kitchen and the television room, where he found his mother lifting the phone from its cradle.

Before she could even look up he started shouting.

"What is your problem?" he said. His mother stared at him, total deer-in-the-headlights startled. "Your life sucks, so you figure mine should suck too? Well, forget it. You're miserable because you let yourself be miserable. You let Dad treat you like crap. You let your boss walk all over you. You let Aunt Judy tell you what a loser you are. You take it

49

all because you like it. If you weren't pissed off about the world, you wouldn't have a damned thing to talk about. So go ahead and bitch about how crappy everything is, and guzzle your gallons of Chianti, but keep me out of it. I didn't do anything but be born. And that's your fault too. So you stay out of my room and stay out of my life until I can bail this crap shack. Then you can have the phone whenever the hell you want, as long as you aren't using it to call me."

His mother broke into tears and dropped the phone.

Jonathan smiled.

But none of that happened. He didn't even get up from his desk. He remained in front of the computer screen, staring at the icon for the song he wanted, knowing it had not had time to finish downloading. His palm still ached from the slap he'd given the desk. His stomach roiled with acid, and his head throbbed.

Screw this, he thought. *Screw it all*.

Bitter night air cut through the collar of his jacket as Jonathan wandered the streets of Warren. He walked past the new housing development they were building next to his apartment complex. More rich people. More kids with high-tech gadgets and high-brow attitudes. Another wave of jerks to shove him or kids like him into lockers. It didn't really matter. Pretty soon Jonathan's family would have to move. The rents would go up like they had in Pierce Valley, and his dad would make them pack up and relocate, this time probably to a smaller apartment. They already lived in Crossroads, the total low-rent section of town. They weren't likely to find anything cheaper unless they moved way out into the sticks. Great. Then he'd never see David. He wouldn't be able to get to work, either. He might have to change schools.

Then he wouldn't even have Emma's smile to get him through the days.

Jonathan turned up the volume on his cheap MP3 player so that music overpowered the depressing voice in his head. Cars raced by. He felt the wind of their passing but couldn't hear them. He didn't *want* to hear anything but feral singing and brutal guitars: a soundtrack for his anger.

He walked through the intersection of Crossroads Boulevard and Periwinkle Street. Five blocks down on the right was his school, a nest for idiots like Toby Skabich and Ox and Cade. *Burn it down*, he thought. *Break it apart with an earthquake and grind the rubble under with bulldozers.* He didn't know of whom he made this request. It didn't matter. Nothing would change. The school would be there tomorrow and the next day and the next. It was like a temple to evil. Even if it fell, the world was full of them.

And evil tastes like candy. Everyone wants a lick.

Twenty minutes later, Jonathan stepped onto the brightly lit sidewalk of the Northside Mall. It wasn't one of those big multi-layered malls like they had in Bellevue or Seattle, subterranean bunkers for the generals of retail. It was flat and quaint with covered walkways lined with shrubs. The mall had a DVD rental shop, a bunch of clothing stores he could never afford, an ice cream parlor where a single scoop cost three-fifty, and a coffee shop, Perky's, the upstanding suburban equivalent of a crack house.

Jonathan peered through the window of Perky's, knowing he didn't have enough change in his pockets for even a small coffee, and he wasn't touching his college-escape money for such a minor pleasure. If he wanted some bean, he'd have to buy it at the Super Stop convenience store down the street.

Inside, Emma O'Neil sat at a table with three other girls. They were in the middle of a really serious conversation, probably about Mr. Weaver. Jonathan imagined walking in and having Emma call him over to the table, but the thought made him suddenly angry.

Why am I wasting my time? She hardly knows I exist. I'm like an extra on a CW drama, and she's the star, and no way are they calling me back for a second episode. It's a stupid crush. Pointless. God, why can't I obsess on a teen pop diva or something? That way, I wouldn't have to see her every day, in the flesh, in the now, in the ridiculous fantasy my stupid head keeps building.

He grew angrier with himself. He couldn't be angry with Emma. She wasn't doing anything wrong. She wasn't mean to him. It wasn't her fault she was perfect and Jonathan was nothing. It wasn't anybody's fault. Life just worked out that way.

Jonathan looked away from her. The next face he saw made him feel no better.

Toby Skabich sat at a small table on the left with Tia Graves. Naturally, she was beautiful in the most predictable of ways, and a cheerleader. They held hands around their massive coffee mugs. Tia was all dreamy eyed, and Toby just kept talking. The perfect teen couple, living the American dream.

Toby never had to worry about his grades, because no teacher would let a star of the football team fail, plus every girl in the school was willing to do his homework if he just flexed his arms or flashed a smile. The tool already had everything—a nice house, a cool Mustang his dad had given him, the best-looking girl in school—but that wasn't enough. Toby wanted more and more. He figured he deserved *everything* and didn't have to do *anything* for it.

Must be nice.

Unable to deal with any more bad feelings, Jonathan turned away from the window.

She sat on a bench in front of the ice-cream parlor. A neon sugar cone glowed above her head, casting her face in shadow. But even with the veil of darkness covering her features, Jonathan recognized Kirsty Sabine.

She wore a long beige trench coat and distressed jeans, nearly white on the thighs. Her head was lowered, chin on her chest, so that her hair draped down either side of her face like frayed curtains.

Had she been there the whole time? Had he somehow missed her when he walked by the shop?

The chill on his neck fanned out over his shoulder blades, and he began to seriously shake. A gust of wind raced down the mall, chasing the sensation, adding to it.

"I couldn't go in either," Kirsty said, not raising her head. She sat thirty feet away, and her voice came to him like a whisper.

A bit creeped out, Jonathan smiled nervously and tried to think of an excuse for why he didn't go into the coffee shop. He didn't want to sound totally low rent by saying something like, "It's too expensive," but he also didn't want to admit his cowardice over entering territory already claimed by Toby Skabich.

"I was just seeing if some friends were inside," he said.

Kirsty nodded her head, a slow movement that

lifted her chin only an inch from her chest before again resting against it.

"I looked in too," she said. "I didn't really like anyone I saw."

"Yeah," Jonathan said. Even though he'd seen Emma, he knew what Kirsty meant.

Kirsty stood, the shadow on her face growing longer as her slight body eclipsed the purple tubes of the neon ice-cream cone. Her beige coat fell neatly on either side of her body, and she brushed the fabric with her hands, smoothing it further. She took a step toward Jonathan and paused. Kirsty looked over her shoulder, into the ice-cream shop, then down the long walk beside it.

Jonathan stepped forward to cover the distance between them.

"Hey," he said, as if they'd just walked into each other a second ago.

"Hi," Kirsty said, smiling and quickly looking away.

Something about her face seemed different tonight, Jonathan thought. Maybe it was the light or lack of it, but her features seemed more fin-ished, seemed almost pretty, something he never would have thought when he saw her in daylight.

"What's up?" he asked, the chill now centered in his stomach. He wasn't used to talking to girls, and it had to be totally obvious to Kirsty. Knowing this only made him more nervous.

"Just out for a walk."

"Yeah, me too."

"My mom's on one of her let's-spend-every-minute-together kicks," Kirsty said. "I couldn't deal, so I bailed."

Jonathan had no idea what it must be like to have a parent insist on spending time with him, but he laughed and nodded his head. "Parents are a pain."

"Total water torture," Kirsty replied. "Every word another drop on my forehead."

They stood quietly for a moment. Jonathan didn't know what else to say to the girl. He was full-on nervous, and the chilled anxiety in his stomach was making him uncomfortable. Maybe he should just say good-bye.

"It's strange so many people are out," Kirsty said.

"Strange?" he asked, grateful she'd broken the silence.

"After Mr. Weaver. I figured most people would

stay home for a while."

"I didn't even think about that. You don't seem too worried. I mean, *you're* out."

"I shouldn't be," she said. "But since Dad left, Mom's been really needy. I figured once we moved, she'd lighten up, but that didn't really happen."

"Sorry to hear about your dad," Jonathan said. The words felt awkward on his tongue. He didn't know Kirsty at all, so his condolence felt insincere. Fortunately she didn't seem to notice.

"Thanks," Kirsty said. "That's nice of you."

"When did he leave?"

"About a year ago. A lot of drama."

"That blows. Do you still see him?"

Kirsty didn't answer immediately. She looked up at the ceiling covering the walkway, stared at it as if searching for the answer there. "Not much," she said, finally. "Like I said, a lot of drama."

Another uncomfortable silence fell over them. Jonathan was about to say "that blows" again, but knew it would sound lame. Instead, he decided to change the subject because it didn't seem like either of them wanted to discuss Kirsty's father any more.

"How do you like it here?" he asked.

Kirsty's response surprised him because she didn't answer his question. Instead, she said, "Do you want to walk? I'm getting kind of cold just standing here."

"I guess," Jonathan said. "Where do you want to go?"

"Would you mind walking me home?" Kirsty said. "It's not far."

"Sure," Jonathan said. It wasn't like he had anything better to do.

Kirsty lived in the Briar Gate development, which was half a mile down Horace Road, the street running parallel to Crossroads Boulevard on the other side of the mall. As they walked, Jonathan found himself unable to relax around Kirsty. Yeah, she was nice, and she was even kind of interesting, but she also seemed distant, sort of cold. Jonathan understood. It wasn't exactly like he was Mr. Personality tonight either. They were simply two school outcasts who bumped into each other and decided to take a walk.

"So, do you miss your friends?"

"Didn't really have friends," Kirsty said. "My dad

scared people off. He'd get up in their faces and drill them like an army sergeant. He was totally paranoid. It freaked people out. I learned pretty young to keep other kids away from the house. And since he was really strict, I didn't get to spend much time away from home, except to go to school and . . ."

"And?" Jonathan asked.

"Church," Kirsty whispered, as if embarrassed. "My folks were both hyper about the church back in Spokane. My mom has totally lightened up about it now, but . . . Ugh! It sucked. What about you?"

"We don't go to church," he said. In fact, he'd probably only been in a church five or six times in his entire life. He attended two Sunday-school classes when he was like six years old, and after that it was just weddings.

"What about friends? I don't see you hanging out with anyone at school."

"My best friend . . ." *Only friend.* ". . . goes to Melling." *And he thinks you're hot*, Jonathan added to himself.

Jeez, what would David say if he found out he was walking Kirsty home? David had played it

totally cool at the bookstore, like he was just goof-
ing about Kirsty, but what if he really liked her?
Would he be pissed or something?

"Was he the guy I saw you with on Saturday?"
Kirsty asked.

"I didn't think you even noticed us. But yeah,
that's David."

"Have you guys been friends a long time?"

"About three years," Jonathan said. "This is the
longest my family has lived anywhere, so it seems
like a long time, but I guess it's not."

Kirsty didn't reply. Instead, she looked upward,
just like she did at the mall. She kept walking, her
eyes directed at the sky.

Again Jonathan noticed she looked almost
pretty, her face bathed in night, certainly not the
eight David suggested but a good, solid seven. And
again he noticed the odd feeling that came to him
when he looked at her. It was almost like he had
forgotten something but was on the verge of
remembering it, a kind of vague recognition.

A gust of wind startled him out of his reverie,
and he returned his attention to the sidewalk.

"What are you looking at?" he asked, because
the silence was getting to him. It was a stupid

question, but he had to say something.

Kirsty lowered her chin and turned to face him. She wore a shy smile. "I'm just looking at the night," she said quietly.

"Oh, okay."

At Kirsty's house, a two-story brick place with big windows in front, they paused on the sidewalk.

"Thanks for walking me home," Kirsty said, sticking out her hand.

Jonathan was relieved to see the gesture. For a couple of heart-stopping seconds, he'd wondered if Kirsty considered this chance meeting a kind of date, wondered if she might expect a kiss or something. He knew that was just his imagination going into hyperdrive during the quiet stretches of their walk, but still, he felt relief knowing nothing was expected of him but a quick joining of the hands.

He took her hand, squeezed lightly, and a shock, like static electricity, crackled along his palm.

Kirsty jumped a little and laughed again. "Magic," she said with a smile.

"Yeah," Jonathan replied, feeling more uncomfortable than he had all night.

"So, you want to get together again sometime?"

Kirsty asked. "For just like coffee or something. Not a date, I mean. It's just good to talk to somebody my own age."

"Sure," Jonathan said, though what he was thinking came closer to *I don't think so*.

"Cool," Kirsty said. "Thanks again for walking me home."

Then she turned away and walked toward her house.

In a second-floor window, Jonathan noticed a silhouette, the dark form of a woman peering out between two white curtains. Kirsty's mother, he assumed.

Still, the shadowy shape unnerved him, just as Kirsty herself had done. He took a step back on the sidewalk. At the end of the path, Kirsty opened her front door and stepped into the dark foyer.

Jonathan turned to walk home. He was already wondering how he would explain this encounter to David.

"You were scammin' on my woman?" David asked, mock anger edging his voice as it rolled over the phone line. "That's cold, brah."

Jonathan laughed. He rolled over on his bed and stared at the ceiling, glad his friend wasn't really upset. "Yeah, well, I'm a chick magnet. They can't stay away."

"Whatever. The important question is what did she think of me?"

"She thinks you're a god. Way out of her league."

"True," David said. "Too true. I knew she was way into me. SWIM, baby, SWIM. So, what's this Kirsty like? Tell me what I'm missing."

That wasn't an easy question. Jonathan still didn't know what to make of the girl. She seemed nice, certainly not a geek, and no way was she stuck up. It was that feeling he had when he was with her—the sense that he was forgetting something—that totally messed with his head. And he knew it was probably just being full-on freaked out by speaking with a member of the opposite sex, a rare occurrence at best. But it wasn't like he thought she was hot. She didn't intimidate him in that way. He didn't really know what to tell David.

He settled for "She's okay, I guess."

"I'm translating that to mean freak, and not the good kind."

"No," Jonathan said. "She's cool. I mean, I was all pissed off with Mom, so I bailed. Then I saw Toby the Scab at Perky's, reminding me why my life sucked so thoroughly. Kirsty just kind of showed up. It wasn't like anything was wrong with her. I just didn't have my mojo flowing."

"Jonny Boy," David said, "you have no mojo. I say that as a friend. You are mojo-impaired. You're mojo-less. You lack da MO . . . JO."

"Like you're any better?"

"I am the Mojo Master. Kiss my ring, bitch."

Jonathan broke up laughing. He could picture David standing in the middle of his room, one hand on a hip and the other extended, palm down, presenting his fingers and a ring.

"You're totally deluded," Jonathan said.

"I paint pretty pictures of an ugly world. So, what's the story? Are you going to ask her out? Is Kirsty going to be Jonathan's she-slave or what?"

"No," he said. "I'm not into her like that."

"Good," David said. "You keep feeding the undying flame of Emma worship, and I'll handle Kirsty. That way you won't get hurt when she realizes she can't live without the David."

"She's all yours."

"All is going according to plan."

"You're disturbed," Jonathan said.

"You don't know the half of it," David replied.

Jonathan lay in bed, staring at the shadows on the ceiling. Unable to sleep, he thought about Kirsty, her plain face somehow more complete, more attractive at night, and he thought about Mr. Weaver. Since Kirsty was in his English lit class with Mr. Weaver (and they did talk about the guy a little), it wasn't a big stretch, this connection. It was, however, strange. In his mind he was walking with Kirsty, listening to her speak: *I couldn't go in either . . . I didn't really like the people I saw . . . My dad scared them away . . . Strange so many people are out . . . after what happened to Mr. Weaver.* Then Jonathan pictured Mr. Weaver in his living room—he had no idea why; he certainly didn't know what the teacher's house looked like— and the pudgy Weaver was watching television, drinking a beer from a tall glass. The next moment Mr. Weaver was gasping silently, clawing at his face. *Strange so many people are out . . .* Then Mr. Weaver was outside, soaring through space, but it wasn't a pleasant flight. He scratched and kicked at the air, his mouth was open as if to scream, but no sound emerged. He hit high up on a tree, his body bending back slightly with the impact. He fell forward, arms and legs dangling, his body perfectly balanced on a thick tree limb.

Jonathan shook the reverie from his mind. It was just too unpleasant, so he decided to think about something else.

That was easy enough.

He thought about Emma O'Neil. Imagined holding her, and this time it wasn't just to comfort her

67

while she mourned their late English teacher. No, what Jonathan imagined was having met Emma by accident at the mall instead of Kirsty. He saw her smiling, almost mischievous face, hanging before the neon tubes of the ice-cream parlor.

She wore the short red skirt she'd worn two Mondays ago, the fabric smooth and tight to her hips. With the skirt she wore a snug white sweater with short sleeves, a top Jonathan had seen her wear half a dozen times, to breathtaking effect. She didn't say anything at first, just looked at him, noticing him. Finally.

Hey, Jonathan said, as he had to Kirsty.

Hi.

What's up?

Just hanging out. I thought I might find you here.

Emma stepped up to Jonathan and wrapped her arms around his neck, leaned in close to place her lips against his.

Even imagining such a moment made Jonathan blush. He smiled to himself.

He shifted in the bed, rolled over to look at the window.

The wonderful image fled, and Jonathan froze.

Eyes open and staring. His heart beating fast.

A man-shaped shadow fell over the glass. Its darkness was deeper than the night. Somehow solid, it was framed between his open curtains. This wasn't simply a shadow though, because Jonathan could make out eyes, nose, and mouth. They seemed painted on the form. They also seemed furious with him. The lips moved silently, their edges low in a disapproving frown. The smoky eyes darted back and forth, scanning the interior of Jonathan's room.

Childhood fears of the bogeyman flooded back. He felt like a little boy, paralyzed by the knowledge that monsters did exist, and they lived close. This wasn't how he pictured the bogeyman, though. It looked more like the robe of the Grim Reaper, inhabited by a spirit instead of a skeleton. Whatever it was, it scared the hell out of him.

He closed his eyes, attempting to blink away this angry phantom, but it remained on the glass. Sweat popped out on Jonathan's neck. His pulse sounded in his head, a staccato thunder.

Against the glass the shadow rippled. It spread out like liquid, smearing the facial features, making them transparent, so Jonathan could see a corner of the apartment complex through the form. With another rippling wave it rose, like a manta ray climbing through an ocean current.

Then it glided skyward and was gone.

Jonathan leaped from the bed. Every muscle and nerve sprang and sparked as if he'd been coiled up for hours. His fingers and toes tingled badly, and his stomach felt as if it were filled with ice water.

"Crap," he said in a high whisper. "Crap. What was that?"

He paced the room, trying to burn off some of his nervous energy, hoping motion would bring some sense, some logical explanation to his frightened mind. He wanted to believe he'd been asleep. It was a dream. A nightmare. A trick of his overactive imagination. But no, he was awake. No foggy remnants of sleep were on him. There had been no moment of time unaccounted for.

He paced faster and ran his hands through his hair, scratching his scalp furiously to release a tingling shower of anxiety down his back.

Tuesdays were always quiet at the bookstore. Usually Jonathan liked it when the place wasn't busy, but tonight the time just seemed to drag. Everything was pretty well stocked and shelved and the few customers roaming through the store apparently knew what they were looking for, because he'd only had one older woman ask him to look up a title: Clive Barker's *Abarat*. They were sold out.

David was acting strange, adding to the night's unease.

On break they sat at the back of the café. David guzzled his coffee and barely said a word. Jonathan knew his friend was distracted, but he also seemed frustrated, like he'd lost his wallet and was trying to figure out where he'd left it.

"What's up with you?" Jonathan asked.

"Mmmm . . . ," David hummed, looking into his nearly empty cup. "Nothing. Just tired."

"Up all night planning world domination?"

"No," David said. "Just had some things to take care of. Didn't sleep much."

Jonathan debated telling David about his own sleepless night. He didn't have a clue how he would explain the shadowy thing in his window. There was no way to without sounding like a total loon, so he kept his mouth shut.

"How was school?" David asked, still looking in his cup.

"Good," Jonathan said. And it was true.

Toby the Scab didn't show up for classes (Tia Graves probably wore him out last night), so Jonathan was spared a locker hug. It was actually kind of funny seeing Ox and Cade in the halls. They saw Jonathan coming, whispered to each other, shrugged. It was like they couldn't figure out what to do to their smaller classmate without Toby's direction. Jonathan found himself grateful for their limited imaginations.

"Did you see Kirsty?" David asked. Now he peered up from his dwindling coffee supply.

"Barely," Jonathan said. "We said 'hey' before class, but I didn't see her the rest of the day."

"Really?" David asked.

His friend sounded cold and annoyed, as if he thought Jonathan was lying to him. *What the hell?*

"Yeah," Jonathan said, cautiously. "*Really*. What's going on, man?"

"Nothing. You're paranoid."

David again looked up at him, or rather past him. For a second David's eyes lit up, then the spark in them was snuffed out. They went cold.

"Your girlfriend is here," he said.

Jonathan turned, expecting to see Emma O'Neil stepping onto the mezzanine. Instead, he saw Kirsty Sabine, walking toward the table. She wore the long beige coat and tight black jeans with a plain white sweatshirt. Her hair was brushed smooth and pulled back into a neat ponytail. She smiled and lifted her hand in a low wave.

Jonathan nodded and said, "Hey."

"Hi," Kirsty said.

It was when Jonathan turned to introduce a pouting David to Kirsty that he understood his friend was totally jealous. He was really into Kirsty, and it pissed him off that Jonathan had spent time with her, even though it was totally random. *Crap!*

"Kirsty, this is my friend, David."

"Hey," David said. "What's up?"

"Just shopping."

The silence that followed, filled with turmoil and discomfort, weighed a few tons, and all of them rested on Jonathan's shoulders like a couple of marble gargoyles. He looked at Kirsty and then back at David, then back at Kirsty, who looked totally confused and suddenly a little embarrassed.

"Do you need some help finding a book?" Jonathan asked. When he heard his own voice, it sounded full-on rude, so he quickly added, "Or do you want to hang here and have some coffee with us? We're only on break for another five minutes, but . . ."

"Coffee sounds good," Kirsty said.

"I'll get it," Jonathan said. "We get a discount."

"Thanks. Black is fine."

With that, Jonathan walked away, and the gargoyles shifted a bit on his shoulders, felt slightly less heavy. Maybe David and Kirsty would hit it off or David might discover he wasn't really interested in her. Jonathan had to do something. David was his only friend, and there was no way he was going to sacrifice that, especially not for a girl he barely knew. Even if he were attracted to her, even if she were Emma O'Neil hot, David was a bud, and you didn't screw a bud over.

Jonathan felt better by the time he got Kirsty's coffee, which was actually free because Myrna, the café cashier, was a burnout and didn't want to calculate the discount and make change. He saw David and Kirsty talking. David was smiling. That was good. Very good.

He put Kirsty's coffee on the table. She thanked him.

"So what are you guys talking about?" he asked.

"David was just telling me how you two met."

"Oh man, don't tell her that," Jonathan said.

"I have to," David explained. "The wheels are already turning and can't be stopped. It's a momentum thing."

"It's an ass thing."

"Perhaps we should let Kirsty decide."

"I want to hear it," she said, grinning from ear to ear. "Unless you'll be totally pissed?"

"Not *totally*," Jonathan said.

"Well then," David announced, "like I said, it was early in the school year, and Jonny Boy here had just transferred in. Back then, all of the cool kids used to go to this place called Coffee. Perky's wasn't open yet, and the place was just a few blocks from the school. In front of Coffee, there was this kind of patio with half a dozen tables, and the Specials—that's what the popular kids call themselves—well, they used to take over that area, and it became this orgy of coffee and cell phones and WiFi, like an office for kids whose job it was to be dickheads. Every day the Specials sent Naomi Mattis ahead to kind of reserve the area."

"I totally forgot about Naomi," Jonathan said. "God, she was their full-on slave. Whatever happened to her?"

"She's at Melling now," David said. "She had about a million dollars' worth of makeover done, and the last operation, which was some kind of chin implant, went wrong. This all happened before I transferred, but people told me she looked totally Resident Evil there for about three months. Everybody slammed on her, but then when her face got fixed, she was excruciatingly hot. So she put together her own group of

Specials, and the nightmare continues."

"So superficial," Kirsty said. "Why do people have to make each other so miserable?"

"Because if people were happy," David said, "advertising wouldn't work."

"Kids would be jerks without advertising," Jonathan put in.

"True," David agreed, arching his eyebrows, giving his round face a strange, surprised expression. "But they now have a hundred new things to be jerks about. Clothes, palm devices, televisions, haircuts, cell phones—even water. If you don't have the latest, you're a loser and therefore a target. Advertisers know it. They want us to be unhappy so we'll buy their crap. It's totally documented. But I digress from my story."

"Our break is just about over," Jonathan said.

"He thinks he's going to be spared," David said right to Kirsty.

She laughed.

"Anyway, the Specials were gathered at Coffee, another typical day for the rich and popular, when who should appear on the sacred patio?"

"Jonathan," Kirsty said.

"Number-one answer," David replied. He lifted

his cup and poured the last drops of coffee onto his tongue before continuing. "He was a gazelle wandering into a pack of lions."

"They call that a pride," Kirsty said. "A group of lions is a pride."

Her remark startled David for a moment. Jonathan could see the confusion flash across his face, and he understood it. David was used to being the smartest guy in the room. He wasn't used to being corrected, and though he didn't seem angry about it, he was certainly perplexed.

"A pride," David said. "Right. A pride. Anyway, Gazelle-Jonny wanders into the Specials' pride. And as they say on *Animal Planet*, there could be only one tragic outcome."

"What happened?" Kirsty asked.

"They tore me apart," Jonathan said, trying to make light of it, though the memory felt fresh and painful. He remembered those strange, cruel faces circling him—Toby Skabich, Ox and Cade, and a dozen others—asking him questions about where he lived, where he got his clothes, what bands he liked. Their expressions varied from mock interest to rude amusement, and under it all Jonathan felt the hostility of the Specials, felt their ridicule and their superiority.

"It was like a game show of abuse," David said, sounding a little too happy about it. "They'd ask him something like 'Where'd you get those shoes,' right? Making it sound like they were really cool shoes and they wanted to buy a pair. Then Jonathan would answer and they'd all break up laughing."

My cousin shops there, Tia Graves said. He loves it because it's close to the trailer park where he lives.

"God, that's so mean," Kirsty whispered.

"Yeah, well, that's what the Specials are all about," David said. "Anyway, next door to Coffee was this electronics store where they got all the new games at least a week before anyone else in town. I'd just picked up one of the *Silent Hill* games and was walking past Coffee when I heard all the laughing. And there was our poor Jonathan literally backed against a wall with all of these kids around him. He looked scared as hell. He was in over his head. We had geometry together, so I knew his name and I said, 'Hey, Jonathan, come on, we're going to be totally late.' He didn't know what to make of that, but he saw his escape and he took it."

"You saved him," Kirsty said.

"I'm a hero like that," David said with a laugh.

"Then what happened?"

"We went home and played *Silent Hill* for about seven hours."

Embarrassed by the story, Jonathan felt the flush on his cheeks. He wanted to talk about something else . . . anything else. "Hey, we're way late getting back to work," he said.

"Stewart's out back having a smoke," David said. "It's all good."

"Nobody says that anymore."

"And yet, it was just said, which totally negates your argument."

David's cell phone rang then. His ringtone, Johnny Cash singing "Hurt," filled the café.

"Hello. Yeah, mom," David said. "Who? . . . No way . . . Are you kidding? What happened? . . . How? . . . No, but Jonathan does. They go to school together . . . Are you sure? . . . Yeah, okay . . . OKAY! I'll come right home after work, don't freak out. You don't have to pick me up . . . Knock it off. Jesus . . . Okay . . . Okay. I'll see you at ten."

David hung up the phone and set it on the table. He looked dazed. He kept blinking like he had something in his eyes, but the corners of his mouth were turned up slightly. It was almost a smile.

"What?" Jonathan asked.

"They just pulled Toby Skabich out of the lake," David said quietly. "It looks like he drowned."

First Mr. Weaver and now Toby, Jonathan thought.

Two of his high-school tormentors—two in a week—were dead. It was just too weird. And Jonathan felt surprisingly bad about it. Toby was a kid, and yeah, he was mean and rude and totally self-absorbed. But he was just a kid. He was familiar, a part of Jonathan's life, albeit a full-on unfortunate part. Same with Mr. Weaver. He was also part of Jonathan's life. A page in a book. A brick in a wall. An element mixed into the formula of Jonathan's being. Now, there was emptiness, the page torn, the brick removed, the formula incomplete.

Jonathan sat on the edge of his bed. His mom was on the phone in the television room, crying to her sister. His dad did *something* again. Jonathan didn't know what it was. He'd stopped paying attention a long time ago.

He stood up from the bed and went to the closed curtains covering his window. He wouldn't pull them back, didn't want to see what nightmare might be waiting beyond the glass. He was nervous. He didn't know what to do or feel.

You thought about killing them.

So what? Everybody thinks about that kind of junk.

You won't be insulted in class again. You'll never get thrown into another locker. Your life just got a whole lot easier.

That doesn't matter.

It's all that matters.

Jonathan shook this disturbing voice from his head. It was late and he should have been trying to sleep, but after the dark phantom the night before and the news about Toby, he'd never get to sleep now. He wanted to take a walk, to get out of the house. His mother's teary voice bled into his room. But outside wasn't safe. Not these days.

Mr. Weaver was murdered and hung over a tree branch.

Toby was murdered . . .

You don't know that. He could have killed himself, put his perfect life behind him.

. . . and dropped in a lake.

It could have been an accident.

But it wasn't an accident, and Jonathan knew it. Tomorrow, maybe the next day, the news would report that Toby had been murdered and discarded in the lake. No accident. No suicide. He knew it.

And he was afraid. Who would be next?

From *The Book of Adrian, Wed. Oct. 12:*
  Look at me. Look at me, the pretty ones shout. Like birds ruffling their colorful feathers to draw attention, those blessed with fine bone and skin parade about as if they controlled the genetic material randomly bestowed upon them. They deride those not so blessed. Express false pity. All the while absorbing adoration like a drug.

  And they need that fix. They long to be wanted. Though unless they approve, they ignore completely the source of this regard, wholly uncaring of the damage total indifference does.

  Isn't that right, Emma?

Thursday morning, Jonathan stood at his locker. It had already been two days since Toby's body was found. Jonathan stared inside at the stack of books and notepads absently, wondering what it was he needed. He felt lost this morning. Distracted. Entering the school was like entering a funeral home, the faces of Toby's mourners surrounding him. Everyone looked so sad. He hadn't attended the candlelight vigil for the boy last night. The service was held at the city park on the far side of the lake, and he had no way to get there. Even if he had managed a ride, he didn't see how he could attend the bully's vigil without feeling like a total hypocrite.

Instead he'd stayed home and studied for tests in geometry and English lit, both of which were being given tomorrow. He'd talked to David on the phone for a while and gone online briefly to look up some information on Shakespeare, but mostly he'd just read through his notes and checked the textbook. Studying hadn't been easy. Concentrating on anything was tough these days.

Mr. Weaver. Toby.

Damn.

"Hey, Jonathan."

The voice broke his reverie, and he turned away from the contents of his locker and faced the first pleasant surprise he'd had in a long time. Emma O'Neil stood next to him.

"H–hey, Emma," he said. With her face so close to his, Jonathan could hardly breathe. She put his mind in shock, made his pulse double.

"Look, I know this is lame," she said, "and I really hate to ask, but you know that test we're having tomorrow?"

"Sure," he said.

"I can't make any sense of my notes," Emma said. Then she laughed and lowered her head, pointing the nest of spiky hair at him. "Okay, the truth is, I didn't take any notes."

Jonathan laughed too loudly and then bit the inside of his cheek to staunch the unflattering tide of chuckles. "It happens," he said.

"Well, I'm not usually such a flake, but after what happened to Mr. Weaver . . . jeez, and then Toby . . . I just couldn't get my head on straight, so I know like nothing about *Macbeth*. I mean, I'm totally good through *Othello*, right? But if I could snag your notes for the last couple of classes, I'd totally owe you one."

"Sure," Jonathan said, already ducking his head back into the locker to find the right notebook. "My notes should be good."

"They'd have to be better than mine," Emma said.

"I just don't answer questions in class," he explained. "I mean I know the material."

"I know you do," Emma said. "That's why I asked. Look, I have to bail, but could you email them to me or something? I could pull it into my PDA, and that would totally help."

A knot formed in Jonathan's throat. He hadn't transferred any information to his computer. It was all handwritten. Besides, he had no idea if he'd be able to get online at home. His mother might be in a mood. Plus he had to work.

"I . . . uh," he muttered. "I just have the handwritten ones."

Emma's smile faltered a bit. A cloud of disappointment passed over her brow. "Well, that's okay."

"I could make some copies in the library and get them to you later."

"Jonathan," Emma said with a laugh, "you're doing me the favor by letting me use your notes. I'm not going to put you through the lameness of sharing your lunch period with a Xerox machine. I can copy them and get them back to you fifth period, if that's okay?"

"Sure," he said, handing her the notebook with his lit notes. "No problem."

"You're the best," Emma said, placing her hand on Jonathan's shoulder. "I owe you a coffee or *ten*."

Then she was rushing away. Jonathan watched her go, dazed. She was so nice. God, she was just so amazing. He leaned back against the lockers and breathed deeply, hardly noticing the throng of kids passing him in the hall on the way to their first period classes.

Was she serious about coffee? he wondered.

No way! he thought, absolutely ecstatic about the idea.

"Well, you're in a good mood," Kirsty Sabine said with a smile, as she veered out of the river of kids to meet Jonathan at his locker.

"Just having a better-than-normal day."

"Nothing wrong with that," she said. "Me too, in fact."

"That's cool."

"Thanks for the coffee the other night. I know I already said it, but you and David were really nice to let me join you. I don't know too many people here, and there isn't exactly a line of kids looking for new friends."

"I know the feeling. I'm glad you could join us."

"David's really cool."

"He's a good guy," Jonathan agreed.

"Are you ready for that test tomorrow?"

"Pretty much. I studied last night because I've got work tonight. What about you?"

"I guess. I never do well on tests. I get all dorky and forget everything." Kirsty paused 'like she wanted to say something else but didn't know how to. Then she smiled and shook her head. "Are you headed to class?" she finally asked.

"Yeah," he said, still buzzing from his conversation with Emma O'Neil. "I guess."

"Well, why don't you walk with me and tell me about David?"

"What do you want to know about David?" Jonathan asked, very pleased to hear the coyness in her voice.

"I don't know. Just stuff."

"I can tell you plenty of *stuff*," Jonathan said, starting into the flow of students. Kirsty followed, clutching her books to her chest, her head cocked toward Jonathan as he prepared to fill her in on David.

The librarian, Mrs. Vierra, found Emma O'Neil's body at the end of fourth period. The elderly librarian, her hair a tight brush of white, had been stacking books and heard a scream and then a clatter in the stairwell. Panicked, she ran onto the landing and looked down to find Emma sprawled below. The books she was carrying, including Jonathan's notebook, were scattered along the stairway. Mrs. Vierra dialed 911 as she raced down the stairs. She knelt by the girl and searched for a pulse but found nothing.

She cast her cell phone aside and began to perform CPR. One minute later, Emma was breathing on her own, though she remained unconscious.

Jonathan heard all of this during fifth period, while he waited for Emma to return his notebook. He'd seen the ambulance outside, heard the kids mumbling their panic as they speculated on whom the vehicle was intended for. When he heard it was for Emma, all of the excitement, the joy of the day, drained out of him as if someone had pulled a plug from his big toe to release the emotions. In fifth period Mr. Lane told them what had happened. He said Emma had fallen down the stairs. He called it an accident.

Jonathan was in no state of mind to believe in accidents.

When he got home from school, he called David, but his friend didn't answer his cell or the home phone. Jonathan felt so miserable—his chest aching as if someone had punched through his ribs to bruise his heart and lungs—he didn't know what to do. Emma. Jesus, it didn't seem real. She was beautiful. She was nice. She played jazz piano and wrote for the school paper. She had spoken to him that morning.

Finally. She had spoken to him, and now this.

Falling down the stairs. Heart stopping. Being brought back to life by old Mrs. Vierra. After Mr. Weaver. After Toby. What the hell was going on?

His mother wasn't home, so Jonathan logged on to his computer and went online. He surfed to Westland High School's website, praying to find news—good news—about Emma. He checked the school's LiveJournal, and while dozens of kids had replied to the subject line ALL OUR PRAYERS FOR EMMA, no one had any new information.

Jonathan went to the page for *The Westie*, the school newspaper. He scrolled through the newest issue until he found Emma's picture by an article she had written about teen dating. He didn't read the article. He looked at her picture, never wanted to stop looking at it.

The tears filled his eyes only a moment later. Everything just hurt too much. The light that carried him through his school days had nearly been put out. It wasn't fair. It wasn't real. Why the hell did everything have to be so bad?

Was life always going to hurt like this?

Jonathan didn't really sleep. He drifted off for an hour or two hours at a time, but the slumber was in no way restful. He kept picturing Emma at the top of the stairs in the library, stumbling, pinwheeling her arms for balance, then crashing downward.

At four twenty-eight he signed on to the high school's website. He checked the LiveJournal. At three twenty, Megan Stevens, whose father was a doctor, had posted.

Thank God! Emma's awake. Dad says she woke up at three and asked for a glass of water. I already told you about the X-rays, no serious damage. So I think we can all breathe a little better. Dad thinks she's going to be okay. Totally okay. Thank God!

"Thank God," is right, Jonathan thought. A night's worth of tension fell from his shoulders. He smiled, even laughed a little with relief. He went over the post again and then again to make sure he had read the note properly, letting the wonderful news sink in and be real.

. . . She's going to be okay. Totally okay.

Jonathan closed his eyes and breathed deeply. He signed off of the Web, shut down his computer, and went to bed.

Friday night Jonathan stood at the counter at Perky's. His father had shown up at home late that afternoon seeming flush with cash. He gave Jonathan forty bucks and told him to "make a night of it."

Some night. All day he'd thought about visiting Emma in the hospital, but fear of embarrassment kept him away. He didn't really know her. They weren't close, no matter how badly he wanted to believe they could be. So he'd struggled with going, talked himself out of it, and then struggled some more. Finally he'd decided to stay away. Her real friends would be visiting; her family would be there. She was okay, and for now that had to be enough.

So he hadn't gone to the hospital, and he didn't know what to do. David already had plans. He was going to dinner with his parents. Jonathan didn't want to go to a movie by himself because that just screamed "loser," and he certainly wasn't going to sit around the house to see his father's good mood cross the finish line. He'd walked down to the outdoor mall and browsed through the DVD store for about an hour, checking out the latest titles. He'd checked out the electronics store, comparing the specs on digital cameras, televisions, PlayStations and X Boxes. Things he couldn't afford—not if he wanted to get out of Warren and away from his parents—but things he definitely wanted.

Then he found himself outside of Perky's. The usual high-school crowd was gathered, with the notable exceptions of Emma and Toby Skabich. Ox and Cade were inside, sharing a small round-topped table with a couple of girls Jonathan didn't recognize.

Whatever, Jonathan thought. Without Toby, Ox and Cade seemed to have become helpless. They were like a snake without a head.

He walked into Perky's and went right up to the counter and ordered himself a mochachino, because he'd always wanted to try one. (*And maybe with the leftover cash I can send flowers to the hospital . . . for Emma.*) The guy behind the counter reminded him of Myrna from Bentley's Bookstore Café. He spoke slowly, his eyes clouded and distant. Maybe all coffee clerks were a little burned out.

Jonathan grabbed his drink and turned from the counter to begin the search for a table. It was unlikely. On Fridays, from the moment school let out until the shop closed, the place was slammed. Kids came and went in shifts. A lot of adults, too. But luck was on his side, and he found a small table in the back shoved against the window, across a narrow alley from the men's room.

The counter blocked his view of Ox and Cade, which meant it blocked their view of him, and Jonathan was happy as hell about that. He pulled a book from his backpack and opened it on the table.

He wouldn't read. The book was a prop. Nothing more. It was weird enough being out on a Friday night. Usually he hung out at David's, watching direct-to-DVD trashy slasher movies. But David had plans. Jonathan was on his own, but he didn't want to just sit in Perky's staring at everyone. So, he pulled out the book.

He'd picked the paperback based on its lurid cover. Something cheesy, so people wouldn't tag him as too brainy. He had no idea what the book was about, just one of the dozen remainders he'd bought cheap from the store and brought home. It didn't matter what it was about, though. It was, after all, just a prop.

Every time he stopped moving, every time he wasn't distracted by conversation or motion, he thought about Emma. Or he thought about the murders.

All week at school, everyone had been in mourning, talking endlessly about how "great" Toby had been. Even the kids he'd picked on joined in the chorus of his coolness. A lot of the kids looked scared, and Jonathan understood that. What he didn't understand was how so many of Toby's victims could suddenly act like they'd lost such a great friend. He felt bad Toby was dead, but he just couldn't bring himself to join his fan club.

He took a sip of his drink and was surprised by how sweet it was. It tasted good and all, but he was used to coffee tasting like coffee. He never used sugar, rarely added milk. The taste so surprised him that he swallowed wrong and started coughing, just about the time Ox appeared over the counter.

Like his name suggested, Ox was huge. His legs were probably bigger around than Jonathan's waist. He had black hair cut short to his head, and his cheeks were stubbled with a five-o'clock shadow that belonged on a guy twice his age. He was dumb and cocky, a typical combination for a high-school hero, but when he saw Jonathan, he looked surprised, even embarrassed. He nodded quickly as he passed, making his way to the restroom.

Jonathan didn't know how to respond, so he dropped his head and pretended to read his book until the men's room door closed. He took another sip of the too-sweet coffee.

When Ox emerged from the men's room,

Jonathan was pretending to read again. He didn't look up, so he was startled when Ox sat down in the chair opposite him.

"Hey," Ox said.

Jonathan was almost too stunned to respond. He closed the book and searched the room over Ox's shoulder, expecting to find Cade barreling down as part of an attack.

"Hey," he replied nervously.

"Good book?" Ox asked.

"There's a lot of blood," Jonathan said, though he had no idea if that was true or not. He thought it sounded dumb enough to impress Ox.

"Cool," Ox said, nodding his head several times after the word had left his lips. He seemed undecided about something, and he did an odd thing with his lips, sucking them in between his teeth as if he was preparing to heft a tremendous weight. "Look," he finally said, "Cade and I were talking earlier, and we feel like crap for what's been going on. Really, man. That locker stuff was Toby's thing. It was just for laughs, you know? But it was totally lame."

Was he apologizing? Jonathan couldn't be sure. He didn't say anything, just watched Ox, who looked at him, then the table, then the floor.

"It's like nothing against you or anything," Ox said. "It's just something we did . . . for laughs, right? I don't want you to think we have anything against *you*. I mean, it was Toby's deal. Cade and I were just always there."

"Yeah," Jonathan said. *You were always there. Laughing. High-fiving like a pack of morons. No. Like a* pride *of morons*, he thought.

"It's like, I can't believe he's gone. You know?"

"Sorry," Jonathan said. It seemed like the right response, but it felt awkward on his tongue.

"Yeah. Thanks. You're a cool guy. I guess I kind of always knew that," Ox said. "You're a bit scrawny, but a good guy."

Ox was trying to make a joke. Jonathan forced a smile, still thinking the monstrous kid was a dick-head, but maybe a lower-level dickhead than he'd once believed.

"Thanks, man," Jonathan replied.

"So, we're cool?" Ox asked.

"Sure."

"Cool," Ox said rapping the table with one of his giant hands. "Yeah. Okay. Cool. I gotta get back over there. I just . . . okay. Cool."

Ox stood. He appeared confused about which way to walk. He leaned toward Jonathan, who flinched. Ox rapped him lightly on the shoulder. A friendly gesture. Then he turned and made his way around the counter, leaving Jonathan stunned, confused, and relieved.

What the hell is going on? he wondered. Were things actually getting better for him?

Then he lifted his drink for another sip and paused with a cloud of whipped cream against his lip.

Kirsty Sabine walked into the coffee house.

And David was holding the door for her.

Jonathan looked down at his book, pretending to read. He felt awkward, though there was no reason for it. David had lied to him. His best friend said he was having dinner with his folks, when he was actually on a date with Kirsty. So why did *he*, Jonathan, feel guilty, like *he* was intruding or spying on them?

This was lame. So lame.

"Busted," David said, dropping into the chair across from him.

Jonathan looked up, startled. Disappointment

in his friend set his nerves on edge. He tried to play it cool, but it felt like he'd shake apart at any moment.

"Hey," he said, closing the book and setting it down. "What's up?"

David looked over his shoulder and then leaned his arms on the table. "I got a date."

"Doesn't look like your parents," Jonathan said, trying to sound amused.

"I know," David said. He laughed. "Thank God, right?"

"So what's with the blatant untruth?"

"Yeah, sorry about that. I didn't want you giving me a hard time about it. I mean, if we went out, and she didn't groove on the magic that is me, I didn't want it to be a thing, you know?"

No, Jonathan thought. He didn't know, but he wasn't going to get up in David's grill over it. His best friend looked too happy for him to try and spoil it. David's round face was glowing, his smile wider than Jonathan had seen in a long time. He liked seeing his friend having such a good time, but the lie still gnawed at him.

"So, how's it going?" Jonathan asked. "Is she groovin' on your girth?"

"We're cool," David said. Flashes of red rose on his cheeks, and he looked away. "Yeah, we're cool. Full on SHAC."

"Okay," Jonathan said, "what does that mean?"

"She's hot and cool."

"You're just reaching now. SWIM was better."

"Well, I think she actually is, that's the weird thing."

"That's great," Jonathan said. "But you might want to get back over to her before she has time to think about what a grotesque mistake she's made." He grinned and grabbed his coffee.

David rolled his eyes.

Before David could reply, Kirsty walked around the counter. In her hands she held a couple of tall cups of coffee. She looked great. Again, she seemed prettier than Jonathan remembered, though he had seen her in class just that morning. Maybe it was her makeup or the short jacket that revealed more of her figure.

She saw Jonathan and smiled. "David said you were here."

"And here I am."

"I didn't see you when we came in," Kirsty said. She set the coffees on the table. "Can we join you?"

"Sure," Jonathan said, "but I was about to head out."

"Oh, come on," Kirsty said. "You can stay for a few minutes."

Jonathan noticed the expression on David's face—a small smile, tight with annoyance—and knew hanging out wasn't the best idea. He almost agreed to stay, a bit of payback for the lie his friend told him, but he decided not to be a tool.

"Nah," he said. "I should bail."

Kirsty looked genuinely sad he was leaving, and Jonathan wondered if maybe she wasn't having as good a time as David. Then he decided she was just being nice to him. He slid the paperback off the table and fitted it into his jacket pocket.

"You two can take the table if you want," he said, standing up.

"Wait," Kirsty said. She fished in the pocket of her jacket and retrieved a thin flip phone. "I want a picture."

David laughed. "We just bought that thing," he said.

"I'm glad David was with me," Kirsty said. "I was gonna get this totally crappy one. I mean, I don't know anything about these things. They're all the same to me, but he thought this one was a lot better."

"It's got more features," David said, his voice edged with pride. "And it didn't cost much more."

"Okay," Kirsty said lifting the phone in front of her face. "David first."

"You already took three of me outside," David said.

Jonathan could tell his friend was playing it cool. He liked that Kirsty wanted pictures of him. David's posture straightened, and he ran a hand along his hair just over his ear.

"Smile," Kirsty said.

"Ack!" David protested playfully.

Kirsty looked at the phone screen and pushed a button. Jonathan heard a dull click.

"Oh, that's a good one," Kirsty said. "Now Jonathan."

He gazed at Kirsty, again struck by how good she looked. He tried to smile, but it felt heavy on his face. He didn't know if he could hold it. Seeing David and Kirsty together made his chest tingle. What if these two really liked each other? David had lied about his date, tried to hide it. David blew him off, and Jonathan knew it wasn't the last time.

It couldn't be. David and Kirsty would spend time together, maybe a lot of time. Jonathan looked at his best friend, his only friend, and wondered exactly how much their lives were going to change.

Click.

He walked along the sidewalk, the paperback in his jacket pocket, knocking against his hip. He felt miserable. Oh, he was glad for David. It was cool he and Kirsty had hooked up. But scenes from the future flooded Jonathan's mind, scenes that showed him alone, sitting in his bedroom doing nothing. He pictured David and Kirsty sitting on the sofa in David's basement, playing PS3 or just BS'ing the night away. He wasn't in those scenes, and it hurt deep in his chest. In fact, it was the same ache he felt when he heard about Emma O'Neil. It was a sensation of loss, and it was just too familiar.

A brisk wind ran over him. Jonathan stopped

and took a heavy breath. It helped the pain in his chest, but only for a moment. Soon enough the pain returned, like a hard block of burning coal against his ribs.

"Crap," he said with a sigh.

A horn blared at his back, and Jonathan jumped as a massive Ram pickup pulled to the curb ahead of him. He recognized the red truck immediately; it was Cade's pride and joy. Through the back window, he saw two heads in silhouette. An oncoming pair of headlights spread milky glare over the glass, making the heads look like they'd been cut from black cardboard.

"Oh, great," Jonathan said under his breath. The Roid Patrol. Or rather, what was left of them.

He dropped his head and kept walking, pretending not to notice the ginormous vehicle idling beside him. When Ox spoke to him, Jonathan looked up slowly.

"You need a ride or something?" Ox asked. His thick stubble looked even fuller out here, his broad face darker, but he seemed sincere enough. There was no mocking in his eyes, no playful spark that always accompanied his participation in Jonathan's humiliation.

"That's cool," Jonathan said. "I just live down the street."

"Cool," Ox said. "Cade and I were headed out to the hospital to visit Emma. You want to tag? I mean, did you know her?"

"A little," Jonathan said, his stomach knotting at the sound of her name.

"Well, we all want to show our support, right?" Cade asked. "And there's a party after. We're going to have some beers. You should come with. I mean, to show there's no hard feelings or anything."

Jonathan looked into the truck. Ox and Cade had been sitting with a couple of girls at Perky's, but they weren't with them now. Maybe they were already on their way to the party Cade mentioned, or maybe they were at the hospital.

The thought of seeing Emma, of not having to walk into the hospital room alone, excited him. He could see she was okay, maybe bring her something. He still had plenty of money in his pocket. He could buy her flowers in the hospital shop and give them to her. Just a friend thing. If he weren't alone, it wouldn't seem too weird.

The only problem was Ox and Cade. He didn't really want to ride anywhere with them.

"Come on," Cade called from the driver's seat. "Emma will be glad to see you, and the party is gonna rock. There'll be a ton of brew."

"Yeah man," Ox said. "Come on. Toby gave you so much crap, the least we can do is buy you a beer. I mean what else are you gonna do? It's Friday night, and it's just getting started."

"Hells, yeah," Cade called. "You can't go home this early."

Truth was, Jonathan didn't want to go home. At home he'd just sit around thinking about Emma or David and Kirsty. He'd hear his mom bitching to his aunt or yelling at his father, if his father had actually stayed home. Still, he wasn't sure about getting in the truck.

"Maybe I could meet you over there," he said.

"Oh, man," Cade said. "That won't work. The hospital's like an hour's walk from here."

"Look, we gotta roll," Ox said. "I don't know how late visiting hours are. You in?"

"Okay," Jonathan replied, taking a step toward the pickup.

"Yes!" Cade shouted, happily. "Barnes is moving on up."

Ox grinned and pushed the door open for him.

♥   ♥   ♥

109

"What are we doing *here*?" Jonathan asked.

Cade made a left off the main road onto a dirt trail running through the center of a narrow wooded area north of town. The evergreens were lush, and heavy limbs reached down to sweep the top of the pickup like the brushes of a car wash. The ground was hard-packed dirt, filled with pits. Even with the expensive truck's suspension, Jonathan felt every hole and bump beneath the tires.

"We're drinking a beer for Toby," Ox said. "We're going to toast his memory, man. It's like the thing to do. To show our respects? Then we'll hit the hospital to visit Emma."

"It's like bad news first, then good, right?" Cade added.

Great, Jonathan thought. An alarm sounded in the back of his mind, warning him that being out in the woods with his two remaining tormentors was a less than brilliant situation. But Ox and Cade were being cool. They seemed genuinely changed by the fate of their friend.

The Ram made a final lurch, and Cade killed the engine. Next to him, Ox nodded his head earnestly like they were about to view Toby's body in the funeral home or something. The headlights remained on. Tree trunks, pale in the halogen beams, stood like columns holding up the night. At the farthest reach of the light, the edge of the lake lapped gently against the shore.

"In a few days, they'll have those stupid white crosses and all kinds of crap," Cade said, sounding solemn and angry. "They'll build a lame little shrine for him. They'll nail pictures and poems and shit on a tree trunk out here, and some brain-dead cheerleader will leave a stuffed animal, like it means something to him. But that's not Toby, man. Toby wasn't about that stuff. He lived, you know? He surfed it fast and nasty. A blunt. A beer. Jacked up on caf and barreling through the night. He wasn't about flowers or poems."

"Totally," Ox shouted.

"Yeah!" Cade yelled.

Jonathan leaned back, startled by this display. The guys in front of him threw out their fists, connecting with each others' knuckles. Punch it in.

"For Toby," Ox said, throwing open the door of the pickup.

Cade also climbed out of the truck, but Jonathan remained in his seat, unsure of what to do. This seemed like a private moment between a couple of triple-cappuccino-wired first-stringers. He quickly calculated the distance back to his house and figured they were two miles from Crossroads. It would take him at least forty minutes to walk home.

That might not be so bad. Suddenly the idea of attending a party filled with cut-and-paste replicas of Ox and Cade didn't sound terribly fun. And he wondered if visiting Emma was ever really part of the plan. How late were visiting hours?

Before he could make up his mind, Ox leaned into the truck and said, "Come on, Barnes. You're with us now."

"Cool," Jonathan said, and he almost smiled.

He slid toward the door. The phrase "You're with us now" went right to the center of him. At school on Monday, Ox and Cade might pretend he wasn't a part of this night, but right now he was with them, and despite all of the alarms ringing in his head, Jonathan wanted that more than he'd ever admit to himself.

The air outside was icy. A bitter wind blew over the lake. It gained speed as it pushed its way through the tree trunks.

Ox slapped him on the back. The giant was smiling.

Cade met them at the nose of the truck, holding a six-pack of Budweiser. The headlights were still on, projecting their shadows over the woods. Cade's rose up a thick tree trunk on the left, and Ox's flattened out over a low nest of bushes. Jonathan's ran forward, over the dirt trail, a dark facsimile of his shape, stretching out toward the water lapping at the lake's edge.

"It's freezing," Ox said.

"Antifreeze," Cade replied, hefting the six-pack.

"Well, hand one over."

A minute later, they all stood on the shore, looking out at the plum-colored lake. This was the only part of the lakeside that hadn't been developed. Lights ran a ring around its edges, except for a dark patch on the far shore. That was the city park. Two tiny pinpricks of light broke that patch of darkness as a car pulled into the park's drive.

Probably a couple of kids looking for a place to make out, Jonathan thought. *Maybe David and Kirsty.* Then the distant lights went out.

"They found him over there," Ox said, lifting his beer and gesturing to their left. "They said somebody dropped him from high up, like out of a helicopter."

"Totally," Cade said. "They did a full *CSI* episode on his ass, and they like knew he got dropped into the water."

"And he was already dead," Ox added. "No water in his lungs. So it's like, somebody snatched him, right? Then they smothered him like that fat-ass Weaver. Then they hauled him out here and . . . splash!"

"Weaver was way up in a tree," Jonathan said. He sipped from his own beer and the chill made him shiver.

"Right," Cade said. "Right. Now, what kind of a psycho does that? What kind of psycho *can* do that? It's like some supernatural crap. I mean, serial killers don't rent helicopters, and besides, no one saw anything. So, what's up with that?"

"It's not like some psycho threw him or something," Ox said. "I mean, even Cade and I couldn't toss a guy up into a tree or way out into a lake."

"It's weird," Jonathan said, and took another quick sip from his beer. "Shouldn't we be getting to the hospital? I mean . . . you know . . . visiting hours?"

Ox and Cade didn't reply. They just looked at him. Both smiled. They looked like they had just solved some great riddle and were very pleased with themselves.

Cade crushed his beer can in a fist and tossed the litter into the trees. Ox turned and set his on an old stump. Both boys turned to Jonathan, that same satisfied expression carved deep in their faces.

Then the atmosphere on the lakeside changed. Jonathan felt it like another blast of cold air off the lake.

A trap, you idiot. You walked right into a trap. They were never going to visit Emma, and there was never a party. This is your party.

Jonathan backed up a step. He dropped the beer can, and it rolled along the dirt path, leaving a dark trail of spilled fluid in its wake.

"See," Cade said, "Ox and I were wondering exactly how strong someone would have to be to launch a guy like Toby that far out into the water. I mean, to do it hard enough for one of those cop doctors to notice the damage. Right?"

"Knock it off," Jonathan said.

"Chill out, Barnes," Ox said. "We gave up on the

115

idea about two minutes into it. It's like we don't have any high-tech crap to actually measure that kind of thing."

"Right," Cade said, stepping forward. "We totally gave up the science project. We thought of something better instead."

Jonathan turned to run, but Cade was too fast. He lunged forward and got a handful of Jonathan's coat and shirt. He clamped down on his shoulder painfully and hauled him back. Ox stepped up and grabbed Jonathan by the lapels. Both boys looked down at him, their faces cruel masks in the flood of the headlights behind him.

"We decided to do this for Toby," Ox said. "He would have wanted it this way."

"It's a hell of a lot better than flowers and teddy bears," Cade added.

Panic flared in hot sparks through Jonathan's chest. Christ, what were they going to do to him? One last beating in the name of Toby Skabich? Maybe throw him against a tree a few times to make up for the days they hadn't managed to toss him into a locker?

From their right, a rustling of bushes rose up, and Ox whipped his head around.

"It's just the wind, Numbnuts," Cade said. "Come on, let's do this. It's freezing out here."

Then Jonathan was being lifted off the ground. Cade had his ankles, and Ox slid around to his back, grabbing him under the armpits. They hauled him like a corpse to the water's edge. Jonathan struggled, nearly freed himself of Ox's grip, then realized if he did shake free, he'd only succeed in cracking his head against the trail or maybe a rock.

They were going to throw him into the lake. An offering to their dead friend, a token of their appreciation for Toby's guidance over the years. He taught them to be bullies and now they were showing how well they'd learned the lesson.

"On three?" Cade said, grinning down at Jonathan.

Then he was being rocked, swung in the air. Once the two larger boys had him moving at a good speed, Ox started to count.

"One," he said.

The tree line, the sky and the stars all rocked to the side. Then rolled back. In their center was Cade's cruel face.

"Two," Ox called.

"Don't!" Jonathan said, more frightened by the impending humiliation than the freezing water.

"Three!"

He sailed through the air. Wind cut at his neck and cheeks. His arms flailed out, scrambling to find something to hold on to, anything to stop this. But then he was falling. He hit the water with a crash.

His body went terribly numb as he sank into the lake. A thousand icy needles punctured his skin, and his chest grew so tight from the cold that he felt certain his ribs would crush his racing heart. Frigid water pushed into his nose, stinging his sinuses. His wet clothes acted as weights to drag him down.

Jonathan paddled frantically. He kicked with his legs. A submerged tree branch scraped his ankle. Then his foot hit the muck at the bottom of the lake. The other soon followed. He swatted at the water with all of his strength until he could stand upright. Water cascaded over his face as he broke the surface. He gasped for air, then spit out a mouthful of spray. He brushed back his hair and wiped at his eyes.

His feet were so cold he couldn't feel them anymore.

On the shore Ox and Cade laughed. They punched in another congratulations and followed it quickly with a high five. Both boys retrieved fresh beers and clinked the cans together.

"How's the water, Barnes?" Cade asked, grinning like a lunatic.

Ox toasted the air with his beer can. "For you, Toby." He upended the can and drank deeply. Once finished with that, he stepped forward and poured a stream of beer into the lake. "Drink up, man. Rest in peace."

Then the night came for him.

Jonathan wasn't far from the lake's edge. Ox and Cade had only managed to toss him about ten feet in, but the bottom dropped off quickly and he stood in water up to his chest. He could wade out in a few seconds, and that's what his body wanted to do. It wanted to flee the freezing water, but Jonathan remained where he was, fearing what else Ox and Cade had in store for him should he climb out of the lake.

They stood on the dirt path, lit from behind by the headlights of Cade's Ram truck. They congratulated each other and raised beers up, toasting

Toby the Scab and Jonathan's dunking. They laughed.

Behind them, the headlights dimmed. The brash halogen beams faded until the path was nearly black.

"Battery's dying," Ox said.

"No way," Cade replied.

From where he stood in the lake, Jonathan saw that Cade was right. Something moved over the truck's hood, down its grille to cover the bulbs. It was a sheet of darkness. A shadow with no source, like a piece of night torn from the sky. Like the shadow spirit he'd seen outside his bedroom window.

Reaper, he thought, remembering how the shadow had reminded him of death's theatrical manifestation.

"What the hell is that?" Ox asked.

And then he found out.

The murky form sliding over Cade's truck tore loose and glided over the path. Ox threw an arm up over his face, suddenly blinded by the exposed headlights. Jonathan watched as the Reaper flew, flat and rippling like the flag of some dark country.

"Jesus!" Cade cried, throwing his beer can at the approaching shape.

Ox spun around as if to run into the lake, and the shadow caught him. It fell over his head like a hood. Beneath it, his eyes grew wide and his mouth opened as if to scream. A moment later, he was being hauled off the path, into the air. Ox sailed over the lake, his feet only inches from Jonathan's head. Then, he changed direction and soared back toward the dense woods.

His body hit high against a pine trunk, maybe twenty feet up. The Reaper engulfed him, secured Ox against the tree like a bug in a cocoon. Hands raked the fabric of the shadow. Feet kicked. But Ox couldn't break through.

On the path, Cade screamed. He did a strange dance, making little circles in the dirt. He called out for his friend, but his voice was already heavy with mourning.

A dark shape—another Reaper—raced past Jonathan. It skimmed the surface of the lake. And it wasn't alone. A third slid down the trunk of a tree at Cade's back.

"Look out!" Jonathan cried.

Cade looked up at the branches and saw the

thing coming for him, moving like a stain over the rough bark. He ran and screamed, his voice high and piercing as he charged for his truck. The shadow peeled away from the tree and tore after him.

Jonathan turned in the water, looking over his shoulders, checking his back to make sure no more of the shadowy Reapers came for him. When he turned back, he saw Cade was inside the cab of his truck. Fresh terror flared in Jonathan's chest. That ass was going to leave him here, leave him with these things.

"Cade," he called, hearing the engine roar to life. "Come on, man!" he pleaded.

But Cade was beyond reason. Jonathan could see his terrified face through the windshield, lit up by the cab light. The football player darted his head from side to side, as if trying to figure out how the vehicle worked.

A shadow slid down the windshield like dirty water.

The truck roared again and sped backward down the path. It crashed into a tree a moment later. Then, the truck lurched forward, eased toward Jonathan as Cade turned the wheel, adjusted the tires on the trail.

The truck was gone a minute later, the head-lights receding to dime-sized dots through the trees as Cade escaped the nightmare at the lake's edge. Jonathan looked for Ox in the trees, but it was difficult to find him in the dark. His gaze darted between the tree trunks and the black mouth of the woods. The dirt trail rolled through the chasm like a brown tongue, taunting him.

Jonathan's body shivered violently against the freezing water and the fear. He took a step toward the shore, then paused, looking for the Reapers, knowing he'd never see them coming. But he knew he couldn't just stand there. He could swim, but where? Besides, he'd seen one of the things gliding over the lake, moving fast. If they wanted him, they'd catch him before he made it ten yards.

But they don't want you, a voice whispered in his head. The thought startled him with its cer-tainty.

A tree branch groaned, and its needles hissed. The noise repeated and grew louder. Jonathan snapped his head toward the sound. He saw some-thing moving down the tree. It didn't glide slowly. Rather, it fell and tumbled, hitting branches hard, until it finally crashed into a thatch of bushes at the tree's base.

Ox.

The phantom was done with the bully. It had smothered Ox and discarded his body.

Frantic, Jonathan searched the banks for any of the creatures. His foot slipped in the muck, but he righted himself quickly. Maybe he could hold his breath, escape them under the water. *Then I can drown instead of suffocate.* His mind ran through a catalog of useless ideas. His teeth chattered loudly and his jaw ached from tension.

The desperation built. *Where are they? Where are they? God, what am I going to do?* Helpless and cold, he felt certain he'd cry.

He stood in the lake for another three minutes before his fear and discomfort crystallized into anger. *Enough*, he thought. *Enough.* If they were going to kill him, they could kill him, but he wasn't going to die in this lake like a drowned rat. Jonathan stepped forward, pushing a low wall of water ahead of him. He took another step and then another.

Jonathan emerged from the lake, and a deeper cold, one he couldn't believe existed, wrapped around him. His bones and skin ached under this cold.

"Da-a-a-mn!" he said through chattering teeth.

He stood on the path, dripping, exhausted, and trembling. If the Reapers were going to attack, it would be now.

But they didn't attack. They had come for Ox and Cade, not him.

Jonathan turned into the mouth of the woods. He jogged into the trees, down the uneven dirt path. Then he ran.

No one stopped to give him a ride. Whenever the street lit up with the lights of an approaching car, Jonathan turned with his thumb raised, but the cars just sped by, ignoring him, letting him freeze. He ran until his sides ached, then walked for a while. Then ran. He searched the streets, the sky, the yards for signs of a new attack from the Reapers. His mind raced, but every thought was a spark, a mere firefly dashing through his brain, and there were so many of them. It felt like his head was filled with television static. White noise.

At home he went into the bathroom and stripped off his wet clothes, hung them over the shower rod. He turned on the hot water and climbed in. The spray felt like acid on his skin as the heat confronted the cold that had worked deep into his bones. He stood under the scalding spray for five minutes before adding a touch of cooler water. Then he leaned against the wall and let the shower run over him for another twenty minutes.

He dried himself, went to his room, and put on a pair of sweat pants and a T-shirt. He put on socks because his feet were still cold. Then he climbed under the covers, pulled them tight to his chin, and stared at the ceiling.

He didn't even think of turning off the over-head light.

The first thing he did the next morning was call Bentley Books and tell Stewart he was sick and wouldn't be in today. Stewart acted like he didn't believe Jonathan's story, but Jonathan didn't really care what the manager thought. No way was he leaving the apartment. After the call he gathered up his clothes from the bathroom and walked down the hall to the utility closet. Dropped all of the garments, still damp, into the washer. He poured detergent over them and turned on the machine.

In his room he sat at his desk. He needed to write things down, to make sense of them. He reached to turn on his computer, then paused.

If he wrote his thoughts on the computer, they might be retrieved. David told him once that nothing was ever really erased from a computer. Jonathan didn't know if this was true. It sounded impossible, but his fear and paranoia were so great, he wasn't going to take the chance. What if the police questioned Cade, and he told them about Jonathan being there? They might come to question him, might take his computer. They could misinterpret something. They could blame him for Ox and Toby and Mr. Weaver. It was nuts, but it was possible.

He pushed the computer keyboard out of his way. On a plain sheet of copy paper, Jonathan began to write.

Can't go to the police. What would I tell them? They wouldn't believe a thing I said. Reapers? Crap. Cade could tell them, but they'd think we both killed Ox and made up some crazy story. Mr. Weaver. Toby. Ox. What about Emma? Did

*those things attack her? Knock her down
the stairs? She had no permanent damage,
so why did Mrs. Vierra have to perform
CPR? Why wasn't Emma breathing?*

*This is about me. It's totally mental, but
I know it's about me. But who? It can't
be David. Yeah, he digs horror movies
and supernatural video games, but so
do a billion kids. They're just games.
They aren't real. But who else would do
this? Who else could do this? Kirsty? This
was her first year. The trouble started
when she came to school. But why? She
doesn't even know me. Not really. Why
would she do this? People are dead.
David is smart. He could have found
something in a book. He had that book.
That occult history book. He said it was
for a class, but what if . . . David saved
me before. When the Specials had me
cornered at Coffee. He showed up and
got me out of there. David would try to
help me. Wouldn't he see killing these
bullies as helping me? What about
Emma, though? She never hurt me.*

Maybe it was just an accident. This is all crazy. David wouldn't kill anybody. He's my best friend. He's not psycho. I'd totally know if he was psycho.
I have to figure this out.

Jonathan turned the sheet over. He shook out his hand. He needed all of these thoughts out of his head. He needed to make sense of things or else he'd never be able to stop it.

Magic. Witchcraft. These things aren't just appearing on their own. They have a purpose. If it were random, I'd be dead. They'd have killed me in the lake. What are they? Ghosts? Demons? Something else? They wrap around a person. They hold them until the person suffocates. They must be strong. Strong enough to hold Ox. Strong enough to lift him twenty feet off the ground. They tried to get Cade, but he locked himself in his truck. They couldn't get to him, couldn't magically pass through the glass or the door. They are solid ... I think. Is Cade

still alive? Did he go to the police? Would
the police believe anything he said?
Would he blame me? Jesus, he'd probably
blame me. The cops would know I couldn't
do that to Ox. I'm not strong enough.
They'd know that, wouldn't they?
What if I am doing this?
Maybe I have some power I don't even
know about. Is that possible? Is it me?
No. It can't be. It's about me but I'm not
doing this. Am I?
No. No. NO!
It's David. Or it's Kirsty.
It has to be.

Jonathan flipped the paper over and read it from the beginning. He let the words sink in, and they helped untangle his thoughts.

David.

Kirsty.

He stood from his desk and took the paper with him. In the kitchen, he lit the edge with one of his mother's matches and watched the sheet burn. He dropped it in the sink and kept his eye on the paper as it blackened and curled. Once it

131

was reduced to ash against the metal basin, he turned on the water and doused the char. With a paper towel, he scooped the mess out of the sink and threw it in the trash.

"Where are you?" David asked.

Jonathan sat in the living room, ears peeled in case his mother returned.

"Something happened last night," Jonathan said. "Can you talk?"

"Yeah. I'm hiding in the poetry section. It's totally empty. So what happened?"

"I can't really get into it right now, not over the phone."

"Then calling me about it seems kind of point-less," David said, humored.

"It's not about that. Well, it is, but not exactly. We need to talk. Can I come by your place when you get off work?"

"Can't," David said. "I'm on stud duty. The woman and I are seeing a movie."

"Kirsty?" Jonathan asked.

"She's the only one for now."

"David, we have to talk before you guys go out."

"I already know the facts of life, Jonny Boy,

but thanks for offering."

"David, I'm serious. Damn serious."

There was a long silence. Jonathan thought David had hung up on him, but a deep breath, like a sigh scratched through the speaker at his ear.

"Hey? You there?" Jonathan asked.

"Yeah, I'm here," David said. "Look, I figured something like this would happen."

"What are you talking about?"

"TAJ, man," David said, as if it was obvious. "Total ass-faced jealousy. You figure that now that Kirsty and I are together, you're going to get frozen out. Like we won't hang anymore or something. It's totally not like that. I mean, we can't be kids for . . ."

"Ox was murdered last night," Jonathan said to shut his friend up. "Okay? I saw it. He and Cade dragged me down to the lake. They decided to memorialize Toby by throwing me in. Then . . ." He didn't know how much he could say without sounding completely nuts, but he had to convince David. "These things came out of the woods. I couldn't see them real well. They just showed up. They chased Cade off, but they killed Ox. They left his body in the bushes by the lake."

"No way," David said. "You saw it?"

"Yeah," Jonathan said. He struggled against the memory of Ox being engulfed and yanked into the air by a black sheet. "I saw it."

"Did you call the cops?"

"I couldn't. I don't know how to explain it to them. It's all really screwed up."

"You said 'things' came out of the woods?"

"I can't explain it," Jonathan repeated. "Not over the phone."

"So, what does this have to do with Kirsty?"

"It's just a feeling I've got. It all started happening this year, after she started school."

"You don't even know her," David said, suddenly on the defensive.

"I know. But she's like always there. She saw what these guys were doing. I can't think of anyone else," Jonathan said. *Unless it's you.*

"Apparently Special K isn't just for breakfast anymore."

"I'm not high, David."

"You have to be. Think about it, Jonathan. A girl you don't even know is going around and killing people because they pick on you? Does that sound balanced? Does that sound even remotely two plus two? I mean . . . Jesus . . . it's not like she's dating *you*!"

"David, listen . . ."

"I can't believe you're being such a dick about this. Look, man, it's not my fault you don't have other friends. Okay? It sucks, but it isn't my fault. Kirsty and I are having a good time, and you feel left out. Well, tough. I can't believe you'd make up this kind of crap just to get in the middle of it."

"I'm not making anything up."

"Then you're nuts. You're paranoid and deluded, and you need to get yourself some meds. And Jonathan, don't you dare try to implicate Kirsty in any of your paranoid crap. Okay? I'm warning you. Just keep your mouth shut, or you're asking for a whole lot of trouble."

"Are you threatening me?" Jonathan asked.

"Just don't push me, Jonathan."

The phone line went dead.

From *The Book of Adrian, Mon. Oct. 17*

Knowing whom to trust is like the fable of the two doors. Behind one door is a paradise, lush with comfort and sustenance; beyond the other is a ravenous tiger, aching to rend flesh and fill her belly. Every person one meets is a door—do they offer safety or savagery?

Given time, we could erode the door's surface and peer through to see what awaits us. Friends may be exposed as false. Those who first seem to be enemies may be revealed as saviors. But what if there is no time and a door must be chosen? In such situations we are at the mercy of fate—the 50/50 chance that our trust will be wasted and our lives further damaged.

Isn't that right, Jonathan?

Saturday afternoon Jonathan dozed on his bed. Groggy and exhausted but too frightened to actually fall asleep, he tried to rationalize the conversation with David, tried to see it as anything but a threat. He couldn't. Not really. Every time he thought about David's words—*"Just don't push me, Jonathan"*—he pictured Ox being smothered against the trunk of a tree. The two things were inexplicably connected in his mind.

When the phone rang, he was drifting down into a shallow sleep. The noise startled him, sent his heart to ticking like a stopwatch. He looked around his room, confused at first as the remnants of sleep crept from his head. The phone rang again.

David? Let it be David. I don't want to believe what I believe.

"Hello?"

"Barnes?" The voice was quiet and nervous, but

it wasn't David's. It was Cade Cason's.

"Good-bye," Jonathan said.

"Come on, man. I just want to talk for a minute."

"Leave me alone, Cade."

"Fine," Cade said. "If that's what you want. We're cool, right?"

"Whatever," Jonathan said. "Just stay out of my face."

"But we're cool, right?" Cade sounded desperate like a henchman trying to please his master. "I did what you told me, man. So I want to make sure we're cool."

Did what I told him?

"Just tell me what you want."

"Yeah. Right," Cade said, all but babbling. "It's just. I mean . . . Is it cool to talk?"

"Go ahead."

"Yeah. It's just that after last night, I got to thinking, and you totally don't have to worry. I didn't tell anyone anything. Okay? I mean, maybe you're right, and Ox had it coming."

"I didn't say that," Jonathan said, disgusted by the implication. Ox was murdered. No one deserved that, no matter how much of a jerk they were.

"Whatever, okay? The thing is, I think we can help each other. Right?"

"Help each other?"

"Right. I mean you don't really fit in at school or anything, and I can totally help with that. No one's going to bust your ass anymore, okay? You can hang with me, and I'll introduce you to the Specials, and things'll be cool."

Jonathan listened to Cade's prattle. With everything that was going on, did Cade really think Jonathan was interested in popularity?

"And it's not like you have to do anything," Cade said. "I mean . . . it's just . . . I've got this uncle, right? And you know, he lives alone and stuff. But he's full-on Hilton rich. I'm way up in his will, okay? So, I'm thinking if something happened to him, we could both make out good."

Jonathan wasn't sure he was hearing Cade right. Was he really asking him to commit murder? Was Cade that sick?

He thinks I controlled the things that killed Ox, and now he wants me to kill his uncle so he can inherit the guy's money.

"Are you insane?"

"Dude, I'd totally cut you in. Right? I mean, it's

not like the police are going to be able to put this together or anything. Those things are untraceable. And I turn eighteen in like a month, so it's not one of those trust-fund things I can't touch."

"Jesus," he hissed.

"Look, dude, I know it's full-on cold-blooded, but think about it. We'd be set for life, and he's a total ass. I mean it. He's like a seriously unkind bitch."

Sickened by Cade's proposal, Jonathan pulled the phone from his ear and was about to hang up when he remembered something Cade said.

"You said you did what I told you?" Jonathan asked.

"Totally, man. I haven't said a word about Ox to anyone."

"When did I tell you this?"

Cade laughed nervously. "What do you mean? Last night, man. When you called to tell me to keep quiet."

"Okay, Cade. But the thing is, I didn't call."

"Dude, it's cool," Cade said. "We're tight, okay? You don't have to screw around with that mysterious stuff anymore. I mean nobody else was out there last night. We're the only ones that saw what happened, and I'm totally keeping it quiet like you said. So we're cool."

"I don't know what you're talking about."

"Right," Cade said with a laugh. He didn't believe Jonathan at all. "Where'd you come up with that name, anyhow? It's cool."

"What name?"

"Adrian," Cade said.

Adrian? Who the hell was Adrian?

"I don't know anyone named Adrian," Jonathan said evenly.

The phone line was silent for several heartbeats as Cade processed Jonathan's words. "You're telling me you didn't call last night?"

"Did the caller sound like me?" Jonathan asked.

"I don't know, man. You disguised your voice."

"But it was a guy?" Jonathan asked, desperate for an answer. *David?*

"Damn," Cade said. "I wasn't supposed to say anything. I'm screwed. I'm so screwed. He said I shouldn't say anything. Oh God. I gotta get out of here."

"Cade," Jonathan said. "Are you sure it was a guy?"

But the phone line was already dead.

"Just don't push me, Jonathan."

The rest of the weekend passed in a blur. Jonathan didn't sleep for more than thirty minutes at a time. Late Saturday night, he went to his room and pushed a wad of dirty clothes against the bottom of his door, imagining far too clearly a Reaper slipping through the crack and coming for him. This small accommodation to his fear did little. Whenever he closed his eyes, he pictured dark forms swarming over his small apartment, flitting through the living room and down the halls. Sliding like oil over the roof shingles and along the carpet. He thought about David and his friend's words. He knew it was a threat, but he didn't want to believe David was suggesting Jonathan might follow Mr. Weaver or Toby or . . . Then he pictured Ox again, smothered by one of the phantoms and being dragged through the air. Jonathan would wake with a start, look around the room quickly for any sign of movement, then get out of bed and pace the floor. He'd check the window, check the pile of clothes at the foot of his door.

Once he was back in bed, it started all over again.

He walked through Sunday like a zombie, barely able to keep a coherent thought, though he tried. He struggled to make sense of what he knew, but his sleep-deprived brain punked out on him. Just as he would latch onto a thread of logic, a Reaper would flit through his mind and snatch it away.

David didn't call him, and he was afraid to call David.

Jonathan watched the news. Ox was considered missing. So was Cade Cason, but there was a difference. The police were searching for Ox because the boy's parents were frantic—he hadn't come home Friday night. The police searched for Cade because they wanted to question him about his friend's disappearance.

"We have reason to believe Cason has left the area," an old guy in a police uniform said during a press conference. "If you have any information about his whereabouts, contact authorities at . . ."

Cade had split town. Bailed. Jonathan figured that wasn't such a bad idea.

But they'd find him. Cade wasn't smart enough to stay on the run long. The police would catch up to him. In a few days, a week at most, Cade would be sitting in an interrogation room, babbling about that night by the lake.

Jonathan didn't have a clue what he'd say to the police when they came for him. It was just something else to worry about, something else to keep sleep away.

Sunday night was no better than Saturday, and when he came out of his final nightmare Monday morning, Jonathan felt like his body had been beaten by a hundred sticks. His head ached and felt packed with cotton. His limbs weighed too much, and he struggled to get out of bed.

He had to go to school, he thought. If any place was safe, it would be school.

His completely weary mind forgot that it hadn't been safe for Emma.

The morning sun was too bright. Jonathan's eyes stung from the glare as he trudged along the sidewalk. When he passed the mall, he paused, looked at Perky's, wondered why he wanted to look at the place, and then continued on. His head throbbed. His stomach churned with acid. It would have been a good day to stay home. It wasn't like he could pay attention to anything his teachers said for more than a second or two anyway. Except he didn't want to stay home. He couldn't take another minute in the apartment or in his room, which was thick with his fear.

Someone called his name, and Jonathan ignored it because he figured it was just one of the many voices in his head, taunting him with some new nightmare he had yet to imagine.

"Jonathan!" the voice came again. "Jonathan, please wait."

The voice was high, hitting his eardrums with a sharp edge. He stopped walking and shook his head to clear it of the voice—a girl's voice. Emma?

"Jonathan!"

He turned, and his throat closed tight, seeing Kirsty Sabine running down the sidewalk toward him. He blinked in an attempt to clear the cottony haze falling over the girl. In doing this, he saw how scared she looked.

"Hey!" Jonathan said, searching Kirsty's face and finding himself intrigued by the expression of dread she wore. "What are you doing?"

"You can't go to school," she said rapidly. "Neither of us can. He'll look for us there."

"What are you talking about?"

"David," she said, her voice cracking horribly as if she might cry. "He's so angry. I don't know what he might do."

"I don't understand."

"He tried to kill me," she said. "Last night. God, it was a nightmare. He just freaked out. He seemed so sweet. But . . . but . . ."

David? Tried to kill her?

He wished he could be surprised. As the miserable weekend passed, he had grown more and more certain of David's guilt. It was awful but unavoidable. He didn't want to believe his best friend was capable of such horrible actions, so he clung to the idea that Kirsty was the bringer of evil. But he couldn't believe it anymore. Not after David's threat. Not after Cade's phone call.

"What are we going to do?" she asked. She grabbed Jonathan's jacket tightly and pulled him close. "Where are we going to go?"

"Just calm down," Jonathan said, unable to take his own advice. His nerves were lit. They flickered and flared like tiny fires throughout his body. "Tell me what happened. Start at the beginning."

"We have to get inside," Kirsty said. "We can't stay out here."

"Okay," he said. "Just calm down."

They couldn't go to his house yet. His mother was home for at least another hour, and the last thing he needed was a scene with her. She didn't care if he went to school or not; he was pretty sure about that. But she'd see his truancy as an excuse to ride his ass, and it might get ugly. Could they go somewhere public? Like the mall or Perky's? He wasn't sure. A cop might hassle them. Whenever he'd ditched class before, he had gone over to David's to play Resident Evil or Tomb Raider. That was not an option.

"I don't know where to go," Jonathan said.

"We can go to my house," Kirsty said.

Jonathan had never been in a home like Kirsty's before. David's family had money and a high-tech approach to decoration. Everything was chrome and steel and glass and stone. Every room in David's house had an electronic gadget, either an LCD television or an expensive sound system or a computer; some rooms had all three. It was like a showroom for Sony and Bose. Kirsty's house was just as large, and the stuff inside probably cost just as much, but it was a totally different kind of house. The walls were painted deep shades of brown and green with swirls of lighter colors to give the surfaces an odd sense of motion. The furniture was big with dark wooden frames and intricately patterned cushions. On either side of the raw brick fireplace, wrought-iron stands held thick cream-colored candles. More candleholders, these of some other metal, lined the mantel. No pictures decorated the walls, no posters, no paintings. Instead, broad tapestries, their images faded with time, ran across the walls.

"It's modern goth," Kirsty said, noticing Jonathan's reaction to the place. "My mom always wanted to live in a castle. Weird, right?"

"It's cool," Jonathan said, and he really thought it was. Despite being on the edge of creepy, the living room looked warm and inviting. Still, he wasn't comfortable, considering the reason he was brought here. "Can you tell me what happened with David?"

Kirsty looked sadly at the floor. She nodded her head slowly as if agreeing to take medicine she despised.

"We went out together, just grabbed some dinner at Pan Pacific, you know? We were talking about school, and he wanted to know all about where I used to live and about my family and stuff. And it was really nice. He's totally funny and smart. After dinner we took a walk. We were going to Perky's for a coffee and some dessert, and while we were walking he started asking me all of this off-the-wall stuff, like 'Is anyone at school bothering you?' 'Are your teachers cool?' And I told him everything was fine. Then he said, 'Well if anyone's giving you a hard time, just let me know. I'm an expert at taking care of assholes.'

"I didn't think much about it. I figured he was just being protective, and it was kind of sweet, but there was something in his voice that was creepy, so I changed the subject. At Perky's I asked him about the stuff he likes, and he got real defensive. He didn't really want to talk about himself at all. Then, out of nowhere, he starts saying how jealous you were of us. He said some terrible things about you, and I got really skeeved out about it. He said you just used him because he has money, and no one else would waste their time on you. It was just so mean. And his eyes were all weird and dark, and he was smiling, but it wasn't a real smile. You know? It wasn't a happy smile at all."

The words sickened Jonathan.

"I'm sorry, but he was just so mean, and he totally seemed to *like* being mean. I wanted to go home, but he just kept on, saying how much he'd done for you and that you were totally ungrateful for it. Said you wanted to split him and me up, because you didn't want him to be happy. And it's not like David and I were a couple or anything. I mean . . . not really. We went out a couple of times, but he was all 'No way that loser is going to break us up. We're too special.' I was too scared to say anything. But then he said something like, 'I know you'll be grateful for what I can do. Nobody else is going to treat you the way I can. You're not that hot.' And *that* was totally it. My dad used to make fun of the way I looked. He used to call me names, and after he left, I swore no one was going to do that to me again.

"So I told David I didn't want to see him anymore. I tried to be nice about it, but I was really pissed at him. He tried to talk me out of it, started acting sweet again, but no way was I going to fall for that."

"You said he tried to kill you?"

"Yes," Kirsty said distantly. "At least I think so. I don't know. It's really crazy."

"You saw them," Jonathan said. "You saw those shadow ghosts."

Kirsty straightened up as if startled. Her eyes lit as she stared at him. "You've seen them? My God, I thought I was going crazy."

"You're not crazy," Jonathan assured. "I've seen them a couple of times. I call them Reapers. I watched one murder Ox."

"Ox is dead?" Kirsty asked.

"It's been all over the news that he's missing."

"I haven't been watching," Kirsty said, her voice high with panic. "Oh no. No. No. Then David *is* doing this."

"What do you mean?"

"He followed me out of Perky's, still trying to get me to stay with him, right? He apologized a bunch of times and grabbed my arm and swore he'd be cool, and I was just so upset, I kept saying, 'Leave me alone.'

"He got really angry then. He said I should know better than to piss him off. Bad things happened to people that pissed him off. And he said if I didn't believe him, I should ask Ox. It was a total threat. I didn't get it because I didn't know about Ox."

Jonathan left his place at the doorjamb and crossed the room. He put his arm around Kirsty, who was now very near tears. "It's okay. You're okay."

Kirsty pushed in close to Jonathan, resting her

152

head on his chest. "I was so scared," she whispered. She sniffed quietly and snuggled her cheek against him. "I walked home. I was on Dalrymple about to turn onto Remington, when I heard this weird sound, like a flag snapping in the wind. I looked up and saw these shadows, but they weren't really shadows because there was nothing in the sky to cause them. They were just dark smears in the night, and the only reason I could see them at all was because the stars weren't as bright behind them.

"Then I saw that one of them had a face. A terrible face. It looked like it was in so much pain. And it looked angry. I screamed. I totally screamed my head off and started running. I knew I wouldn't make it home, though. So I ran to the closest house, and one of those things slid up my back. It felt cold and moist, like a slug or something, and I totally freaked out. I fainted and woke up on the sofa of a family named Myers. They called my mom, and she came to pick me up."

"God, you were so lucky," Jonathan said, wondering if fainting had saved Kirsty's life or if something else had spared her the suffocating embrace of the Reapers. "You shouldn't have even left the house today," he said.

"I know, but when I came out of it, and that family was staring at me, I figured I'd just scared myself. I thought it was all some kind of hallucination, or maybe a nightmare I had after fainting. I was so confused; I just didn't know what to think.

"I woke up this morning thinking it was all just a mind screw, but as soon as I got outside, I started getting scared. I started to think about Mr. Weaver and Toby and I wondered if what David said was real. I mean, can he really control these things? I thought if anyone knew, you would."

"I didn't know he could do this," Jonathan said. "Killing people? I mean even if I thought he could work magic, I'd never have thought he could actually kill someone."

It was impossible, a tiny voice in the back of his mind whispered. *This is* David *you're talking about.*

"Well, maybe it isn't him," Kirsty said, pulling away from Jonathan. "Maybe he was just trying to scare me because I hurt his feelings. Boys do weird stuff. Like when they're being rejected, their egos get all crazy. It might not be him at all."

"It's him," Jonathan said, the sickness in his

stomach turning hard and cold. David had hurt Emma and killed at least three people. It didn't seem real, but it was. "Now we just have to figure out how to stop him."

"We have to check the doors and the windows," Kirsty said. "If one of those things got in here, we'd never even see it."

Jonathan looked around the room and had to agree with her. The walls were too dark; the textured paint on them would provide excellent camouflage for those things. He followed her through the house, checking windows and doors, making sure the house was sealed tight from basement to roof.

"When's your mom get home?" Jonathan asked.

They stood outside a door on the second floor of the house. Kirsty paused with her hand on the knob. "My room's a mess, okay?" she said, not answering his question. "Can you wait here?"

"Sure," Jonathan said.

Kirsty slipped through the door and closed it quickly behind her. He leaned against the wall and looked at the door. The knob was made of iron, more of a handle than a doorknob. The door itself looked heavy, not one of those cheap plywood things he had at home. That was good. If those things got in, they couldn't just break the door in. But Jonathan looked along the frame and down, and he didn't like what he saw. A wide gap, nearly half an inch, separated the bottom of the door from the floor. These things, the Reapers, were flat. Could they slip through a hole that size? He wasn't sure, but he didn't want to take any chances.

When Kirsty emerged from her room, Jonathan said, "We're going to need a few things."

They sat on the sofa in the living room. Jonathan stared at the fireplace. He'd made sure the flue was closed, but the hole in the wall made him nervous. On the cushion next to him, Kirsty spun a roll of duct tape on two fingers. Next to her was a bag that held towels, two flashlights, a hammer, some nails, and Kirsty's cell phone. It was an emergency kit. Jonathan figured they could use these things, and he didn't want to have to search the house if they needed them fast.

"You never told me when your mother would be home," Jonathan said.

"Well, that's the other thing," Kirsty said. "She's gone for a few days on business. I couldn't tell her about those . . . those things. God, I didn't want her to go, but I didn't know what to say to make her stay. So I'm alone."

"You're not alone," Jonathan said.

"I would be, without you," she replied. "What are we going to do, Jonathan? We can't hide in here forever."

"I know," he said. But he honestly didn't know what they could do. It wasn't like they could just kill David.

"Why don't we run away?" Kirsty suggested. "I've got my car and enough money in the bank. We could just run away. David would never find us."

"We can't do that," Jonathan said, though the idea was appealing. There wasn't anything keeping him here, especially now that his best friend had gone psycho. "David will just hurt other people. We have to stop him."

"How?"

"I don't know. I'm not exactly Harry Potter. I don't know anything about magic or the supernatural, except for crap I've seen in movies."

"Did you ever see anything like this in a movie?"

"No," he admitted. In movies he'd seen vampires, werewolves, mummies, witches, slashers, and a thousand creatures without names, but he'd never come across anything like the Reapers.

"And you have no idea what they are?" she asked.

"Hell no," he said. "Why would I?"

"It's just that you two were such good friends. I thought he might have said something to you, maybe mentioned a book of spells or something."

"A book of spells?" He remembered *The History of the Occult*, remembered David explaining his belief that magic was the first science, the first religion.

"God, I don't know," Kirsty said, her tone angry. "I'm just scared, okay?"

"I know. I'm sorry. I'm scared too."

They sat quietly for a few minutes. Jonathan's

thoughts raced as he tried to figure out what to do. He could try talking to David again, but if he was freaking out before Kirsty dumped him, Jonathan couldn't imagine what David felt now. Besides, if Jonathan admitted what he knew to David, he might become a target himself. Though who was to say he wasn't already? David had snapped. He'd blown a gasket and spun out of control. Three people were dead, and he'd tried to kill Kirsty, and those were only the crimes Jonathan knew about. They couldn't go to the police. What would they say?

Hi, officers. There's a kid who's controlling these ghost things that smother people. And, well, yeah, he's being a pain in the ass so could you maybe arrest him, please? Cool. Thanks.

Kirsty's mother was out of town, and Jonathan's parents might as well be. They didn't give a damn. Hell, if anything happened to him, it would probably take them a week to notice he was gone. Kirsty's suggestion to run away was looking better and better.

"I'm going to talk to David," he decided.

"You can't," Kirsty said, clutching his arm. The roll of tape she'd been spinning flew from her fin-

160

gers and rolled across the floor. "He'll kill you."

"I'll meet him after school," Jonathan said. "There'll be like a thousand people around. He won't try anything. I'll tell him what I know. I won't say anything about seeing you. I'll just tell him I figured it out, and he has to stop. I'll threaten to go to the cops or something. I mean, he can't get away with this. I can't *let* him get away with it."

"But what if he won't stop? He's got to know the police won't believe you. I wouldn't believe it myself, except . . ."

"I can't let him get away with it," Jonathan repeated. "I just can't."

As the day wore on, Jonathan's nerves grew raw. Kirsty fixed them a lunch of chicken soup and roast-beef sandwiches, but Jonathan just nibbled at the bread and sipped a few spoonfuls of broth.

"I can fix something else," Kirsty said.

"No. This is great. I'm just not hungry."

"When I'm nervous, all I can think about is food, especially Twinkies."

"Why Twinkies?"

"I used to eat them by the boxful, but I was a total cow back then."

"Really?" Jonathan asked. "You used to be over-weight?"

"Total understatement. I was a whale. My dad used to call me Hog."

162

"What an ass."

"Again, total understatement. He couldn't smile unless someone else in the room was crying. He criticized everything I did. Hated everything I wore. Nothing was good enough for him. He once grounded me for a week because I didn't set the table the way he wanted me to. I used water glasses instead of wineglasses or something. I was like six."

"Man, that blows."

Jonathan thought about his own parents. Their indifference was so total, they didn't even bother to comment on his report cards. His mother acted like signing the stupid thing was an act of total martyrdom. His dad just wasn't around.

"So your dad just left?" he asked.

"Not *just* left. He had to make sure me and Mom were good and miserable before he went. One night he sat us both down in the living room and told us that he was unhappy, and it was our fault. He said he couldn't take any more disappointment in his life and thought it best to just leave, because he didn't think we'd ever be the quality of people he wanted to associate with. That's exactly how he put it. We weren't the *quality of people* he wanted to be with, so he was

163

leaving, and we wouldn't hear from him and we had no one to blame but ourselves."

"Jesus, what a tool," Jonathan said.

"After he left, Mom had a full-on breakdown. I mean, she kept buying self-help books and writing these long essays about how we could improve ourselves as people, and she'd make me read these things. It was like it never occurred to her that maybe Dad was the screwed-up one. She totally pissed me off there for a while. I mean, when she wasn't crying over the jerk's leaving, she was all hyped up about projects that would make us better people. She had time-management programs, and she tried to get me to learn French and Spanish. She seemed to be over it for a while. I mean, she still watched every move I made, wanted to be sure I was acting appropriately, but a lot of the weird crap stopped. Then last night she started in again."

"What happened last night?"

"Oh, I made the mistake of telling her about David."

"She didn't like him?"

"Are you kidding? He's like a genius from a wealthy family. She wanted me to marry him, and she's never even met him. She freaked when I told her that we broke up. You'd have thought I'd just told her I'd guzzled a glassful of poison, and she thought David was the only antidote."

"Well, I know he really liked you," Jonathan offered.

"I liked him, too," Kirsty said.

Her response sounded like a reflex to Jonathan, not really heartfelt, but he understood. After all, she'd only known David for a few days. It was natural for Kirsty to be confused about how she felt. Jonathan knew the feeling well.

"I wish I knew how all of this happened," Jonathan said.

"Maybe he'll tell you."

Maybe, Jonathan thought. But he was afraid to ask.

Jonathan drifted out of sleep and was startled by the sensation of being covered. Smothered. A Reaper had come for him in his sleep. Desperate to be free, he rolled, but the thing wrapped more tightly around him. He couldn't breathe. It was all over him, surrounding his head. Jonathan kicked, but his feet were tangled in the fabric of the thing.

He swung out with an arm, but it was pinned between his body and the back of the sofa. He tried the other arm and felt the material give. Finally, opening his eyes, he saw the blanket covering him and threw it on the floor. His chest heaved for air, as if he'd genuinely been suffocating.

He looked around, confused by the strange room. The walls were painted a deep brown. The furniture was old and heavy with intricately patterned cushions. Two wrought-iron stands held candles by a large brick fireplace.

His waking mind raced, trying to figure out where he was and how he'd gotten there. Then he remembered: *Kirsty's house.*

Jonathan sat up, rubbing the sleep from his eyes. A cool film of sweat covered his neck, and his pores felt oily.

"You're awake," Kirsty said.

He turned toward the voice and saw Kirsty sitting in a high-backed chair. Had she been sitting there long? Was she watching him sleep?

A cold tingle ran down Jonathan's back.

"What time is it?" he asked.

"It's after five," Kirsty said. "I tried waking you up at three, but you were out cold."

"Damn," Jonathan said, knowing he'd missed his chance to confront David at school. He could see through the curtains that it was already getting dark outside. If he wanted to speak to David, he would have to go to his house. At night.

"You must have been exhausted."

"Yeah," he said, still groggy. "I guess I haven't been sleeping much lately. It must have caught up with me."

"Do you want some coffee? I made some."

"Sure," Jonathan said. "Yeah, please."

After Kirsty left the room, he blinked his eyes rapidly and yawned. When he stood, the room tilted to the left, then rocked back to the right. Jonathan took a deep breath and waited for the room to level off. He yawned again.

Kirsty returned and handed him a mug of coffee. It was rich and tasted wonderful. Immediately his head cleared. The remnants of his exhaustion faded.

"I'm sorry," he said. "For falling asleep."

"It's okay. You've been through so much." Kirsty put her hand on Jonathan's back. She rubbed slow circles over his shoulder blade. "You can talk to David tomorrow."

"No," he said. "We really shouldn't wait. After coffee, I'll head over to his house."

"That's really brave," Kirsty said. She leaned her head on his shoulder; her hand continued to rub his back.

The scent of Kirsty's shampoo, a mix of almond and vanilla, filled his nose. He drank more of the coffee and stared at the red carpet. The moment confused him. She was touching him, leaning on him for comfort. Part of his mind was in a full-on panic, and it sent waves of unease through his body. But another part of his mind liked this contact. Needed it. It was warm, and he didn't want it to stop.

"Can you stay here tonight?" Kirsty asked.

The question surprised him. He immediately thought she was making a romantic advance, but that was more his fault than hers. He was so lost in the wonderful moment of contact that he'd forgotten, just for a second, what was happening around them. Kirsty wasn't inviting him to her bed. She was afraid of being alone.

"Let me see what David says," Jonathan told her. He finished his coffee with one last gulp and put his mug on the cocktail table. He stood up, already feeling the loss of Kirsty's body next to his. "We might want to go to a hotel or something. Someplace with a lot of people around. We can figure it out when I get back, but I better head over there."

Kirsty stood up too. She wrapped her arms around Jonathan and pulled him close. She kissed him lightly on the mouth, sending sparks of excitement through his body.

"For luck," she told him.

Jonathan smiled and held her hand. Together they walked across the living room and into the foyer. At the front door, he let go of her palm and said, "I'll be back as soon as I can."

"Be careful," Kirsty said. "You don't know what he might do."

Jonathan nodded. He opened the door.

Next to him Kirsty gasped.

David stood on the sidewalk only fifty feet away. Shock and anger covered his face like a terrible mask.

High above his head, three Reapers soared in gentle circles, barely visible against the night sky.

"I knew it," David said.

The heavy kid stomped toward them, but Jonathan was already stepping back, slamming the front door. Kirsty lunged forward and turned the locks. Her trembling fingers fumbled with the chain. Twice, she failed to fit the metal knob into the clasp. Finally Jonathan moved her aside and quickly slid the chain into place.

David pounded on the door. "Kirsty!" he shouted.

"David," Jonathan said. "You have to stop this."

"Shut your damn mouth, you back-stabbing dickhead. I want to talk to Kirsty."

"Go away, David," Kirsty said, her voice cracking with fear.

"Just let me talk to you," David pleaded through the door.

"Come on, man," Jonathan said. "Just stop. You're acting crazy. You can't keep doing this."

"Shut up!" David roared. "She was my girlfriend. Mine. You had no right to do this. Christ, after all I've done for you, you pull something like this? It's SAW, man. Totally SAW. How could you? How could you do that to a friend? *To your best friend?* You didn't even like her. You only want Emma."

Jonathan looked at Kirsty. A flash of hurt played over her frightened expression. She lowered her head.

"Kirsty," Jonathan whispered.

"It's okay," she said, not looking at him. "I already knew that."

"Kirsty! Open the door. Come on. I just want to talk."

Jonathan turned to Kirsty and grasped her shoulders. "You have to call the police," he said. "Just tell them someone is trying to break in, okay?"

Kirsty nodded her head slowly and eased out of his grasp. Jonathan returned his attention to the door. "David," he said, "we're calling the police. You have to get out of here."

"I'm not going anywhere."

Jonathan didn't know what else to say. He leaned against the door, feeling miserable. He was jacked up on adrenaline, but he also felt bitter sadness. His best friend was a killer, a murderer with dark powers. No matter what else happened, his best friend was gone. The realization hurt worse than anything he could remember.

A touch at his shoulder startled him, and he spun to find Kirsty.

"He did something to the phones," she said. "There's no dial tone. Just static."

"You're going to be sorry," David said through the door.

Kirsty ran into the living room. Concerned, Jonathan followed and found her standing at the window, holding an edge of the curtain back.

"He's leaving," she said.

"What about those things?"

"They're still out there."

"Okay," Jonathan said. "Grab the emergency kit. We'd better get ready for a fight."

Jonathan pulled a fireplace poker from its rack. He tested the weight in his hand and slashed it through the air once, like a swordsman preparing to duel. Kirsty grabbed the bag from the floor and checked through its contents.

"Do we have the duct tape?" Jonathan asked.

"Yeah. It's here on top."

"Okay, do you guys have a basement? Some-place without windows?"

"The basement has windows on two sides. A lot of them, but they're small."

That wouldn't work, Jonathan thought. Likely, these things could creep through just about any space they wanted. They had no bones or muscle to give them bulk.

"What about a closet?" Kirsty asked.

"Too small," Jonathan said. "We might be trapped in there for a long time. What about your room?"

Kirsty's eyes lit up. "No. My mom's room. It has a window, but we can block it. If they manage to get into the bedroom, we can still hide in the bathroom. We might need water or something anyhow."

A window shattered at the back of the house. Jonathan's heart leaped into his throat.

"That's the kitchen," Kirsty whispered. "God, they're in the house."

"Come on," Jonathan said. He put his hand on her lower back and pushed her toward the stairs.

They ran, Jonathan one step behind Kirsty. At the bottom of the stairs, movement caught Jonathan's eye. He turned to look down the hallway. Two of the Reapers glided into the hall from the kitchen. They rippled and spun as if caught in a violent ocean tide. But they continued forward, jostling for space in the narrow hall.

"Run!" Jonathan yelled.

They pounded up the stairs. On the landing Jonathan turned with the poker raised above his head, ready to bring it down on the attacking phantoms, but he didn't see them. He scanned the foyer with his eyes and tried to hear the rippling of their bodies through the thundering pulse in his ears.

Jonathan noticed a broad stain beside the front door. It looked like someone had splashed a bucket of water on the wall. Except the stain moved. It pulsed and shimmied, moving slowly upward. Jonathan stepped back.

Another Reaper peeled away from the wall above the staircase only three feet from him.

Jonathan stumbled back as a grin spread over the creature's transparent face. Jonathan spun quickly, using the momentum of his misstep to drive him down the hall. At the end of the hall, Kirsty stood in an open doorway. She called his name, waved for him to hurry.

Not looking back, Jonathan sprinted toward her. Something cold and moist ran over his neck, and Jonathan raced even faster, driven forward by revulsion and fear. As he neared the threshold, he lunged forward. He tossed the poker ahead of him and dove into the room. Behind him, he heard the thwack of the door being slammed.

He hit the floor hard. Pain flared from his hip to his ankle and back again. But he had no time to entertain minor injuries. Jonathan rolled over and got to his knees. He turned and crawled toward the bag sitting on the floor next to Kirsty. He pulled out the duct tape and tore a long strip free. Above him Kirsty was talking, babbling about something, but he was too panicked to listen. He fixed the strip of tape over the gap between the door and the wooden floor. Then he dug in the bag for one of the bath towels. He rolled it up and slid it tight to the door.

With more tape he secured the towel.

"Here," he said, handing the roll of tape to Kirsty. "Seal up the edges of the door. I'm going to find something to wedge against that towel."

The frantic girl did as she was told, but Kirsty's fear was so great and her hands so affected by that fear, she kept sticking the tape to itself. She muttered and swore at her own clumsiness. Across the room Jonathan found a wooden dressing bench. It was barely more than a frame with a cushion but the wood was solid and heavy. He tossed the cushion on the floor and carried the bench across the room. He set the top of the bench on the floor and slid it tight against the towel.

Two minutes later, the door was sealed with ragged strips of duct tape, running around the edges and framing the door in gray. Jonathan checked the seal at the bottom—tape, towel, tape, bench. It should hold, but he had no idea how strong the Reapers were. They could obviously break glass. He had to hope they wouldn't be able to leverage themselves under the door with any real force.

"Okay, now the window."

"How did you know what things to put in that

emergency kit?" Kirsty asked. She sounded awestruck. "I mean, they were exactly the things we needed."

"I spent three nights awake, thinking about these things," Jonathan said. "I imagined a dozen different ways they could get into a house or a room or a car. I guess my imagination paid off for once. Now, let's figure out what to do about the window."

The window would be tough. It was five feet across and at least four feet high. They might be able to wedge the mattress from the bed in the space, but Jonathan didn't think so. Besides, even if they got it up there, they had nothing to hold it in place. No way tape was going to work on that.

He searched the room hoping to find something that would act as a barrier but found nothing. The dresser was too heavy and not big enough. The walls were bare except for another one of those faded tapestries, and it was too small as well. The only things big enough to cover the window were the blankets, the sheets, and a set of beige curtains hanging from a wrought-iron rod.

So that's what they used.

"Can you hand me the hammer and nails?" Jonathan asked.

Kirsty lifted the emergency bag and hurried to close the distance between them. Jonathan took the hammer and a box of nails from it. He hated standing near the window, felt that at any moment it could burst inward, but he was lucky. It took him three minutes to nail the curtains over the window frame and another five to repeat the process with the duvet and a heavy woolen blanket. The barrier wouldn't keep those things out, not in the long run, but it would slow them down. It should be enough. All he and Kirsty needed were a few seconds to get into the bathroom and lock the door.

Once the window was as secure as he could make it, Jonathan returned to the door and checked it. Nothing seemed to have been disturbed. So far . . . so good.

"What do we do now?" Kirsty asked, still by the window, holding the emergency kit.

"That depends on what they do next," he said. "For now I guess we wait."

❦   ❦   ❦

Everything was so quiet.

Jonathan sat with Kirsty on the bed. Every few minutes he rose and checked the door to make sure the seal was holding. He kept the fireplace poker in his hand, taking comfort in its weight.

"What time is it?" he whispered.

"Almost ten," Kirsty said. "We've been in here for hours. Do you think they're gone?"

"There's no way to know. We should probably stay here until morning."

Kirsty scooted closer to Jonathan. Her hip touched his, and he looked at her, trying to smile. *It's okay*, he wanted his expression to say. *We'll be okay*. He put his arm around her shoulder and squeezed lightly.

"I'm just so glad you're here," Kirsty said.

She leaned closer to him until their noses nearly touched. Then they were kissing. The action surprised Jonathan, but he didn't resist. He pressed his lips to hers, felt the softness and the warmth of her mouth. When her tongue flicked out, running over his, Jonathan responded in kind. He let go of the fireplace poker and wrapped his arms around her. She twisted slightly on the bed to accommodate the embrace and pushed her body against his. Electric charges flared throughout his body, sending his nerves to dancing. His thoughts melted, and he let himself get lost in the feeling of her body. For a brief moment, all of the dread and panic of the night slipped away.

But it was only a moment. Though he hated to end the embrace, practical thoughts flooded back, demanding his attention. They had to stay alert.

Jonathan ended the kiss and eased Kirsty away from him. She looked at him with happy confusion and tried to lean in for another kiss, but he held her shoulders. "I should check the door," he said.

Kirsty nodded her head and scooted back on the bed. At the door Jonathan knelt down and checked the tape. It was holding, but he stayed at the door anyway, pretending to examine the towel and the bench, even shaking one of the bench legs to test its sturdiness.

He needed to collect his thoughts. Only the night before, Kirsty was dating his best friend. Sure, they went the way of Brad and Jen, but it had only been a day, and here she was, making out with him on her mother's bed. Was he just a source of comfort for her? Did she expect more?

He didn't know, but he was pretty certain she was an emotional car crash right now, and he needed to be careful.

Besides, he didn't know how he felt about her. Did he feel any genuine attraction to her at all? It certainly wasn't the kind of thing he felt for Emma, but then that was a fantasy, a dream of love. He couldn't consider that real because he didn't even know Emma. He hardly knew Kirsty. Were his feelings simply the result of the night's confusion?

Jonathan tugged the bench leg again. Then he straightened up. He looked at Kirsty, who had climbed all of the way onto the bed and rested her head on a pillow. Her eyes followed his every move. He walked to the window and ran his hands down the fabric nailed there.

"We'll hear the glass break if they try to get in that way," Kirsty said.

"Yeah," Jonathan replied. "Just checking things out."

Kirsty lay on her back, looking at him. Her hair cascaded over the pillow and one of her shoulders. His eyes followed the strands to her breasts. His eyes lingered there a bit longer than they should have, and he forced himself to look away.

He returned to the bed and sat on the edge, facing the door.

"I think they'd already have gotten in if they could," Kirsty said. She reached up and touched Jonathan's back.

"Probably," he said, not taking his eyes from the door.

"You know," Kirsty said. "I was really hoping you'd ask me out that day I saw you at the bookstore. I mean, I liked David, but I really wanted to spend time with you."

"Really?" Jonathan asked. "Why?"

"We're a lot alike, I think. We're both different from everybody else. I used to look at you in Mr. Weaver's class, and even when he was being a total ass to you, you kept cool. It wasn't like you didn't care he was being mean. It was like you were so used to it, you couldn't bring yourself to feel anything about it anymore. I know what that's like."

"He was a teacher," Jonathan said. "We're just kids. There's nothing we can do, so why bother?"

"You can do a lot," Kirsty said. "You just didn't know it. I mean, look at what you did tonight. You saved me. You knew exactly what to do, and we're safe. If you believed in your own power, you never would have let Mr. Weaver or Toby treat you the way they did."

"So you're saying all of this is a good thing?" Jonathan asked with a laugh.

"I think you're stronger now."

"Yeah, and it only took a few people getting murdered and discovering my best friend was a psycho to do it."

"I didn't know how strong I could be until my father gave my mom and me that speech. It about tore me to pieces to hear all of that vile crap coming out of his mouth, but it was the kind of shock I needed to become someone else. Someone stronger."

Jonathan turned. Kirsty wore an expression so warm and inviting it sent a cascade of emotion through his rib cage.

"It's like, everyone wants you to fit into their life, and they'll pinch and tear and beat you into the shape they want, like you're just a piece of clay. Most people don't even know they're doing it, and most never know it's being done to them. Once you know who you are and what you want—once you find your power—they can't hurt you anymore. But until you find it, life is

183

something you have to endure."

He understood what she was saying. Variations on the thought had teased his mind for years, but he'd never had it so clearly spelled out before. He'd let things happen to him. He'd let other hands mold him, fearing that if he protested, he would be cast out, thrown away. Unfortunately there were so many damn hands molding—teachers, parents, asshole bullies— there was very little of him left.

"So do you think I've found my power?" he asked.

"I think you're about to," Kirsty replied. "You could never use it to protect yourself, but protecting me has shown you it's there."

"Afraid I'm just not seeing it."

"I am," Kirsty said. "I'll help you see it. As long as we're together, you'll always see it."

The word *together* jarred Jonathan out of his thoughts. Were they together now? Did he want them to be?

"You should get some rest," he said. "I'll stay up and keep an eye on things."

Kirsty's face fell slightly, just a flicker of emotion Jonathan couldn't identify.

"Okay," she said. "I'll take the second shift. Wake me up in a few hours."

"Sure," Jonathan said. "Good night."

"'Night."

Jonathan drifted up from a deep sleep. Kirsty had relieved him on watch some time ago, and he'd fallen asleep almost immediately. Now his thoughts swam in the misty remnants of dreams, becoming solid and pulling him higher and higher until he opened his eyes. He rolled over on the bed. The fireplace poker jabbed his side, and he bolted up.

"How long was I out?" he asked.

But no one answered.

The room was empty.

Jonathan leaped from the bed. The rolled towel, bound in strips of gray tape, still clung to the door. But the bench no longer sat against it.

The piece of furniture was pushed to the wall.

"Oh no," he whispered. *Kirsty?*

Jonathan ran to the door and eased it open. Lights burned in the hall. He searched the walls for any dark stains creeping there. But he saw nothing. He opened his mouth to call Kirsty and then thought better of it. She could have gone out to check the house and gotten trapped somewhere by the Reapers. If she heard his voice, she might leave her hideout and walk right into them.

He returned to the bed and retrieved the fireplace poker. In the hall he moved quietly, keeping his eyes alert for any motion.

Halfway down the hall he stopped at Kirsty's room. With a trembling hand he grasped the handle. It felt cool in his palm. Gently he pushed down and opened the door. Light from the hallway spilled over the threshold. More light poured in through the window.

It was morning.

Jonathan checked the walls and the ceiling, stepped into the room cautiously, and was met with the pungent scent of pine cleanser, though it didn't look like the room had been cleaned in weeks. Kirsty's bed sat to the left. The linens were rumpled, and various articles of clothing lay amid the sheets and blankets. Dozens of magazines, empty diet cola cans, and assorted papers littered the floor. Kirsty's desk stood to the right, next to a closet with folding doors. It too was messy, but something on its surface caught Jonathan's eye, drew him closer.

His face stared back at him.

Amid the clutter on the desktop sat a pewter goblet the size of a halved softball. A photograph of Jonathan leaned against the cup. He crossed the room slowly, checking over his shoulder with every second step. He leaned the fireplace poker against the desk and lifted the picture.

A thick, foul liquid coated the bottom of the photo. Drops of the liquid dripped from the paper's edge, splashing the desktop.

It was the shot Kirsty had taken of him at Perky's the night of her first date with David. She'd taken the picture with her cell phone, but what was the crap staining the lower quarter of it? Jonathan looked into the goblet and found a low pool of the foul fluid inside.

What the hell?

Jonathan put the picture down. Behind the

goblet was a low stack of similar photographs. These too were stained, much more so than his own picture. In fact, the damage to these photos was so advanced that the faces in them were barely visible through great smears of charcoal-gray filth. The picture on top was of a woman, but her features were impossible to make out through the dismal muck. The second picture was of a man, but here too, the face was obscured.

The third picture, another man, made Jonathan's throat close tight. Even if he had not been able to make out the dull, flat features of the guy through the stain, he would have recognized the cheap blue sweater-vest anywhere.

Mr. Weaver.

The letterman jacket and Denver Broncos baseball cap in the next photo were clearly Ox's.

The next picture he recognized immediately, and he grew furious. It was the same picture he'd found on the school paper's website. He'd cried looking at it. Emma O'Neil's heart-shaped face was covered in a slime of dark fluid.

Jonathan dropped the pictures on the desk and backed away.

Kirsty?

It had been Kirsty all along. Jesus, she'd tricked him. She'd trapped him in her home.

Jonathan turned to the open door, expecting to find her there, smiling evilly at him. But the doorway was empty.

His racing thoughts collided, making it difficult to think. He had to get out. But no. If he fled now, she'd just send her Reapers for him. He needed to find something he could use to stop her. No way was he letting her get away with this.

A spell book?

Kirsty had mentioned something like this yesterday. He'd thought it a really weird bit of information for her to have. Was that the source of her power? Did she have such a book?

Jonathan searched the desk. He found a low pile of textbooks, checked each of them to make sure no occult text was hidden beneath a familiar cover. At the bottom of the pile, he found a leather-bound book and snatched it from the desk. He opened to the first page:

The Book of Adrian.

He read bits and pieces, but the book wasn't filled with mystic spells and incantations. It was a diary. As he thumbed through the pages, a photograph slipped out and drifted to the desk. He snatched it up.

The girl in the photograph was the saddest image Jonathan had ever seen. Her obese body was crammed into a pale yellow summer dress. Stringy hair drooped from her head like oily threads. Her plump cheeks were smeared with rouge. The girl tried to smile for the camera, but she looked like she might burst into tears at any moment. Her suffering was captured as clearly as her homeliness. Jonathan found a note on the back of the photo. It was written in a delicate, elegant print:

Let the transformation begin.

Though barely recognizable, the girl in the photo was Kirsty. Jonathan knew it would be, but he still found the realization startling. Even so, the picture wouldn't help him, and neither would the journal.

He left the desk and made a slow turn, taking in the entirety of the room. When he came around to face the closet, he was again assaulted by the stench of pine cleanser.

He grasped the handles of the closet and threw them back.

"Oh my God." He gagged.

A woman lay across the back of the closet. She wore a blue nightdress and one white slipper. The other slipper sat in the middle of the closet floor. Her eyes stared wide—desperately, eternally. Her mouth was twisted open in a final scream. Jonathan took a step back and noticed two small plastic buckets on the closet floor. This was the source of the sickening pine odor. Kirsty had filled the buckets with cleanser to cover the far grosser stench of a dead body.

"She wanted me to stop," Kirsty said.

Jonathan spun around and found the girl in the doorway. She held two mugs in her hands. Gently she eased the door open farther with her shoulder and walked into the room. Her expression was absolutely blank.

"She said no boy was worth it. But she didn't know. She didn't understand. She'd never met you."

"Me?" Jonathan whispered through a clenching throat. "What in the hell does this have to do with me?"

"I love you, of course," Kirsty said. She walked past him to the desk and set the mugs down. "I told you, we're a lot alike. I knew it from the first moment I saw you."

"We're nothing alike," Jonathan said. "I could never . . . Jesus, you killed all of those people."

"I did it for us," Kirsty said. "You needed to find your power before you could accept mine."

"I don't accept anything."

"When I saw you, I felt we were the same. I've always had the talent, met other girls and a few women that can wield it, but you're the first gifted boy I've met."

"I don't know what you're talking about."

"You will," Kirsty said.

She walked up to him, and Jonathan tried to back away. The contents of Kirsty's closet kept him from retreating farther. Her hands snaked out, palms sliding up his chest like serpents.

"Your old life is gone, Jonathan. Even David. You don't have anyone but me."

Jonathan thought about his best friend and felt sick. He should have known David wasn't capable of hurting anyone. It was Kirsty. Always Kirsty.

"Just accept it," she said, her lips spreading into a dreamy smile. "Together we can do anything. We can have anything we want. I could do it on my

193

own, but it would be so much better together. No one can hurt us. You know it's true. I showed you."

"Emma never did a thing to me, and she certainly never hurt you."

"David told me how you felt about her the first time he called. She was a problem. A problem I intend to solve when all of this is done."

"You're sick."

Kirsty's eyes grew dark. Her smile disappeared to be replaced by a ragged smirk.

"Maybe," she said, removing her hands from him and stepping away. "But I spent sixteen years playing a sniveling victim. I believed every bitch that called me ugly and said I was nothing. I believed my father when he called me a disgrace, a disappointment. And I believed my mother when she told me I needed to get used to the world's cruelty. I believed all of that until I discovered the Talent. Once I did, I proved them wrong. And then I saw you. So much like I was a year ago. Unpopular. Unattractive. Unwanted. But under the surface, I saw this well of power you had no idea existed."

"You're out of your mind," Jonathan said. "You have to stop this. You're killing people."

"They deserve to die."

"No, they don't."

"Oh, come on, Jonathan. You're telling me you never thought about killing those assholes? You did think it. I know you did."

"It doesn't matter what I *thought*! Everyone has screwed-up thoughts. Only monsters act on them."

"Wrong," Kirsty said. "Gods and goddesses act on them. Monsters are merely their weapons." She walked to the desk and lifted the stained picture of Jonathan from its surface. She held it over the lip of the pewter goblet. "You want to meet my monsters?"

"Do what you want," Jonathan said. "Like you said, I've got nothing left. God knows, anything's better than being with you. I'd say your father had the right idea, leaving you."

"Do you really think he left?" Kirsty asked. "After all of this, do you honestly believe I just let him walk away? The only place he went was to a morgue and then to an oven to roast his damned skin to ashes."

"Well, it's got to be better than seeing your ugly face every single day."

"You son of a bitch!" Kirsty screamed. "No one talks to me like that. NO ONE!"

She dropped the photograph into the goblet and stepped back. She lifted one hand to her chest and recited an incantation.

To Jonathan it sounded like *Du-ay. Mor-ay. Du-ay Tom-ay. Mor-ay. Mor-ay.*

Only then could he act. He'd goaded her, wanting her to perform the spell. He still held the picture of Kirsty in his hand. If he could exchange it for the image of himself in the goblet, her Reapers might be fooled into taking her. It was a long shot, but he knew of no other way to bring an end to this nightmare.

Jonathan ran toward the desk. Kirsty looked startled for a moment, but recovered quickly. She flashed out her hand and raked her fingernails down his face. The pain slowed Jonathan, but it wasn't until she buried her knee in his crotch that he stopped.

He dropped to his knees. Pain like he'd never known exploded through his body, radiating from between his legs with such ugly force, he thought he might vomit. His head blossomed with colors, each one representing a different level of agony.

He slumped forward, clutching himself and gasping for breath.

"Idiot," Kirsty whispered. "You've ruined everything."

Jonathan groaned. His eyes were covered in greasy tears, blurring his vision, but he blinked the moisture away. Behind him he heard Kirsty walking to the other side of the room.

"I loved you," she said. "And this is how you treat me? I loved YOU!"

He managed to roll over and see the girl standing in the far corner of the room. "You call this love?" Jonathan asked.

"No," Kirsty muttered. "I call this . . . over."

The Reapers appeared in the doorway then. They did not pause, but soared into the room. Three of them pushed through the door and unfolded to their full size. They danced in the air above him like circling manta rays, wearing grins on their transparent faces. One swooped down and grazed his aching body with its cold, wet form. Another repeated the move, only this one connected hard with Jonathan's shoulder, sending him onto his back.

The third one dropped to the floor. It crept

over Jonathan's head, leaving a moist trail on his hair and skin. He struggled, threw his hands up to pull the phantom off of him, but it was too strong. A moment later his nose and mouth were covered. He beat at it, tore at it with his fingernails, but the phantom was already lifting him off the floor.

Through the film of the shadowy body, Jonathan watched his own hands flail as he rose off of the carpet. The picture of Kirsty, a rectangular blur, flapped in the air, still held firmly between his fingers. His chest heaved for breath, but the ghost's form filled his nose, his mouth. His pulse thundered like drums in his ears. His heart beat like a speeding train, trying to break through his ribs. Up and up. The phantom lifted him from the floor and dragged him to the ceiling. Another of the Reapers wrapped around his legs.

Together the two monsters carried him around the room. They beat him against the ceiling, then dropped to the floor, skimming over the carpet.

Jonathan's head grew light. His body began to hitch violently as his lungs struggled to draw breath. White flashes appeared in his vision, playing against the dark field covering his eyes.

In a final attempt to save his own life,

Jonathan threw out his hand, reached for anything he could get his fingers on. He was helpless in midair. If he could get on his feet, get some control of any kind ...

He felt wood scrape over his chest and arms. He was being lifted by his feet, dangling upside down. He desperately reached out, and the edge of the desk slid into his palm. He held on with all of his might.

The phantoms continued to climb, and a searing agony flared at Jonathan's shoulder. It felt like his arm would rip out of the socket. But he held on.

Through the shade of the Reaper's body, he saw the goblet on the desk's surface. More lights flashed before his eyes, and his torso clenched miserably. He needed air. Needed it right now.

A low ringing filled his ears. His eyes stung from the secretions on the surface of the ghost, but he could see the goblet. He saw his face looking up at him from it.

Jonathan reached down. He dropped Kirsty's picture in the cup. With his fingers freed of it, he yanked his picture from the foul liquid. He flung it to the floor, and suddenly the grip on his feet was gone and he was falling.

The cowl lifted from his mouth, his nose, his eyes. Jonathan gasped, taking in gulps of sweet air, filling his desperate lungs with oxygen as his mind spun out of control like a broken carnival ride. He rolled onto his back and stared at the ceiling, expecting to see the Reapers regrouping above him, but they didn't appear.

From the far corner of the room, Kirsty began to scream.

But it only lasted for a few seconds before she fell silent.

Jonathan looked in her direction.

The Reapers covered her. They did not lift her from the carpet, the mistake they'd made with Jonathan. No. They covered her like a filmy cocoon, pinning her to the wall. Her face was a mask of terror. Mouth wide. Eyes pushed closed. Unmoving. Shaded darkly by the bodies of her phantoms.

Jonathan sat at Perky's staring at the empty chair on the other side of the table. He stirred his coffee absently, looked out the window at the sun-drenched day. People walked along the mall, holding bags of clothes and electronics and toys and kitchenware. They all seemed so happy, so content with their places in the world.

Jonathan wondered what that felt like. Maybe one day he'd know.

"So, dude," David said, dropping his butt into the empty chair. He set his cup of coffee on the table and leaned forward. "You want to run all of this by me again?"

"What's left to tell?" Jonathan asked. "Kirsty was messed up."

"Yeah. Duh. Got that part of the story. Kirsty was freak salad. That's all LAC—loud and clear. I just can't quite deal with all of this yet."

"You and me both," Jonathan said.

"I just don't know how to feel," David said. "It's like, I really liked her. Right? Then she turns out to be totally *not* what I thought, but I miss who I thought she was. It's like missing a mask or something. Totally weird."

"WITE," Jonathan said.

"Huh?"

"Weird in the extreme," he explained.

David smiled halfheartedly. He looked out the window and then turned from the glass.

"Man," David said. He shook his head and peered into his coffee cup. When he gazed up, he looked supremely serious. "I'm really sorry about everything that happened. I mean, everything with Kirsty. I was acting like a total tool."

"It wasn't your fault. She manipulated us both."

Jonathan left it at that. What he knew—and what he didn't want David to know—was that Kirsty only used David to get closer to Jonathan. She knew he wasn't interested in her, not at first. But by turning Jonathan against David, making him think his friend was a killer, they would come together against him. And that's what happened . . . at least for a while. Kirsty wanted Jonathan isolated, alone. She could have just killed David, but that wouldn't have brought her any closer to Jonathan. If anything, it would have driven him farther away. No. She needed David as a scapegoat, needed to use him and hurt him. She probably would have killed him if Jonathan hadn't stopped her.

Another good reason for Jonathan to feel nothing but relief that she was gone.

"So, what happens now?" David asked.

"Now?" Jonathan asked. "What do you mean?"

"Well, are you all magical like she thought or what?"

Jonathan laughed and lifted his coffee for a sip. He let the liquid sit on his tongue and shook his head. "No. I'm not all magical. The only reason those things went after her instead of me is because I dropped her picture in the goblet when I was trying to take mine out. She worked the magic. I just got lucky."

"Damn," David said. "But like, have you tried anything? Like a spell? I mean, did you find her stash of sorceress gear? Did she have books wrapped in human skin?"

"I only found one book," Jonathan said. "It was her diary. Weird-ass stuff."

"Like what?"

"She called herself Adrian. It was a name she liked. She hated being called Kirsty. She was going through this *great* transformation, and when she finished she was going to emerge as Adrian. It was like a slam against her father, because he hated the name. Adrian was his sister's name, and she was a full-on whack job."

"But didn't she already kill her father?"

"Like you said, freak salad."

"Did you keep it?"

"The diary?" Jonathan asked. "Hell no. I mean, it connected her to the murders. She had these entries with the names of everyone that died. You've seen the news. The cops know she was involved. They may not believe she actually had ghosts killing people, but they know she was responsible."

"They haven't talked to you at all?"

"Yeah, they did," Jonathan said. "But it was just to see if I was alive. They found my name in her diary and my picture at her house, but I think they're done with me. No one saw me at her place except you. They probably have my fingerprints, but what are they going to check them against?"

"So it's over?"

"Yeah, David. It's over."

Life could go on. And it seemed to be getting better. Emma was out of the hospital now. Jonathan called her, totally surprising himself with the gesture. It was nice to hear her sounding so awake and happy. She didn't remember a thing about what happened to her in the library stairwell, and Jonathan figured that was for the best. Emma didn't sound particularly upset at all. She called herself a klutz and laughed. They chatted for over an hour. Before hanging up, she promised to buy him that coffee next Monday after school.

"Are you sure you aren't magical?" David asked.

"What?"

"I don't know, you look different," his friend said. "You look bigger or something."

Jonathan laughed and drank his coffee. "I'm not magical."

But, of course, that was a lie. He'd found a second journal in Kirsty's room. In it were a dozen spells. They were generally very simple. A few ingredients for potions, a few rituals, a few words to speak. Jonathan had spent the last week toying with them, always surprised when they worked. And there was so much more to learn.

Kirsty may not have had many books on magic, but they were out there. Lots of them.

He made a mental note to stop the body-transformation spell for a couple of weeks. He didn't want to draw attention to himself.

"No magic here," Jonathan said. "You'll just have to deal with me the way I am."

EPILOGUE

As the last words of the tale passed out of her mouth, Daphne staggered slightly, closed her eyes and rubbed her temples. It was always draining to be a vehicle for the bone stories, but she never really remembered what it felt like until it happened again, so there was no way to brace herself.

Each time the possibility of freedom was so electrifying, and the story, no matter how horrible, so engrossing, it was easy to lose yourself in it, confuse yourself with the characters, even if they weren't you. For a while, Daphne had even wondered if she was somehow Kirsty, before realizing what a monster the girl had become.

She kept her eyes closed a while, to get her

bearings, but she could hear the others talking. They all felt distant, as if they were in the next room and not right beside her.

"A happy ending for a change," Shirley's high-pitched voice intoned.

"Unless you're one of the dead," Anne muttered back.

Daphne wanted to say something witty in response, but bits of the story clung doggedly to her mind. Why? She always wondered why certain stories appeared to each of them. Even if it wasn't theirs, could they still mean something? Were they reminders? Clues? Warnings?

Still feeling secluded in her own head, she opened her eyes to see Shirley shrug and nervously pick at one fingernail with another. "Well, I didn't really like anyone who was killed, did you? In a way, that makes it okay that they died."

"Fun, even," Anne offered.

Mary looked at them both with disapproval. "I never thought of anyone's pain as enjoyable. Enlightening perhaps, justifiable certainly, but not amusing."

Daphne could barely pay attention. *What was that story really about?* she wondered. *A struggle for power? Not knowing who your friends are? Betrayals?*

"Gotta get your kicks where you can," Anne said, but her voice was strained and her eyes kept darting about. "Every rat for himself, and God against everyone."

Isn't that what we're going through with Anne?

Mary threw her hands out in annoyance. "How can you ever hope to remember who you are if you fail to distinguish yourself from beasts? If we're, as you insist, all animals, what difference could it make *what* our lives were like? Doesn't the mere existence of the bones say different?"

"Just because we're all animals doesn't mean we're the same animal," Anne shot back, but her voice was weak, detached, and Daphne found herself staring.

There's something about you tonight. Something different.

"Funny," Shirley said. "Sometimes I wonder if we never really had an identity and we're just really looking for a story we like enough to *make* our own."

Anne looked like she was going to respond, but

then her eyes flashed back to the door.

Is that it? Was the story trying to warn us about you, Anne?

As if in answer taps came from the hall. Simultaneously, they turned toward the sound.

Shirley's hand went up to her throat. "It couldn't be her, not again."

Mary shook her head and smiled reassuringly, "Hush. It's not nearly loud enough for our hellish guardian. Probably just some real animals, as usual. More rats."

Anne leaned back against the counter, put her hands on the edge, pushed herself up, and sat right next to the bones. "Yeah, we're fine," she said, her voice again trailing off.

No sooner did she get there than she raised her T-shirt from the side and slowly put the hem down atop the bones, covering them. As Daphne saw this, she felt her dread, the story, and the moment all come crashing together.

That's it, then.

"Anne, what are you doing?" Daphne said softly, almost in a whisper.

Mary and Shirley started to turn, to see what Daphne was talking about. But it didn't matter, because just then the thick oak door to the kitchen slammed inward. The force pushing it was great enough to crack the door down the middle. The sound that accompanied it was so harsh, all four girls felt as if their chests had been split open.

Framed in the open doorway, a thick gray mist coiled and writhed. It moved in, around, and over itself, swirling like a hundred ethereal cobras trying to hypnotize their prey. At the center of the maelstrom a thing like a mouth formed, just long enough to utter three short words:

"How . . . dare . . . you . . ."

Daphne was so terrified, she was barely able to turn from the manifesting Headmistress. She had to try to figure out how to hide the bones and escape. Still turning as the temperature rapidly dropped, she caught a glimpse of Mary and Shirley, both paralyzed with fear.

But Anne, Anne was gone—and so were the bones.

With a rush of frigid, fetid air, the mist in the doorway flooded the kitchen. As it came for them, the three wraiths tried to scatter, each screaming:

"No! We're sorry! Please!"

"Quiet, Shirley! Just run!"

"Where's Anne? Where did she take the . . ."

Dark tendrils lashed out, faster than Daphne's last coherent thought:

Anne stole the bones. She knew the Headmistress was coming and she stole the bones.

The sound of their voices, the scraping of their movements, all went silent at the same moment. Atop the stove the rat watched the violent struggle of light and dark. It saw long tentacles of churning smoke snap themselves across the pretty mouths of the three girls, while others twisted their delicate hands and bound their lovely legs.

And then the mass of smoke and spirits disappeared, like a fading shadow, through the doorway. The cracked door slammed shut. For a while, the echo of the thud was the only sound. Briefly it crashed about the kitchen, bouncing between the steel cabinets and tile walls, weaker and weaker as it went.

When the reverberations finally faded, the rat finished nibbling the bit of grit in its claws. The noise was terrifying, and the rat had feared the other creatures that were here might be after its food, the way its fellow rats always were. Once satisfied that the room was quiet again, it set about looking for more. When it found the next big gob of rotted, crusty grease, it let into it with gusto, comforted by the fact that tonight at least, it wouldn't have to share with anyone.

TO BE CONTINUED

DON'T MISS

Food pellets sifted lazily through Chelsea Kaüer's hand. One or two at a time, the rough green-brown nuggets tumbled across her fingers, down into the bowl. As they hit the plastic, she counted them in her head: *38, 39, 40, 41.*

She was being watched. She knew it. Four sets of hungry pink eyes followed her every move. Furry noses pressed against the tank's glass. White whiskers swished across the smooth transparent surface. She pretended not to notice.

63, 64, 65, 66.

Like the pellets in her hand, the pet store rabbits jostled each other, trying to push their way through the glass to reach the food that slowly filled the bowl.

72, 73, 74, 75.

A young voice intruded.

"Excuse me." It was said as if one word: *skews-mee.*

Already uncomfortable in her blue-and-red, one-size-too-small Rhett's Pets vest, Chelsea almost lost count.

Just a customer, she told herself, but still she closed her eyes a second and repeated, *75. 75. 75.*

Or else the food would turn to poison.

Pivoting on her knees toward the source of the voice, she found herself at eye level with a mop of brown curls and pink buttons in the shape of flowers down the center of an adorable purple dress. Toddler cuteness had yet to fade from the small intruder's face, so maybe she was four? Chelsea counted the years—*1, 2, 3, 4*—to keep the little girl from bursting into flames.

"I want to pet a puppy," she said. The standard request.

"Oh. Okay. Do you have a parent here?"

The girl jutted a small, sticky finger toward a dowdy woman near the store entrance, where puppies behind Plexiglas yipped and pranced. Loaded down with shopping bags, she seemed singularly unenchanted. Pete, the shift manager, was in the back room taking inventory, and Holly hadn't shown yet. It was up to Chelsea.

She gave the girl her best Disneyland grin.

"Be there in a minute, okay? I have to finish feeding the rabbits."

The girl nodded, but didn't, as Chelsea had hoped, leave. Chelsea took another handful of food and counted faster, hoping the girl wouldn't notice or question.

138, 139, 140, 141.

She did both.

"Why are you counting? Why don't you just pour it out?"

141. 141. 141.

Chelsea kept the grin plastered on her face but lowered her voice. "I have something called OCD." Before the girl could ask, she added, "It's a kind of sickness in the brain. Sometimes when I'm nervous or tired, it makes me count."

"Are you nervous or tired?"

"Tired."

The cute little brow furrowed. "I count sometimes. It's not a sickness. How does it work?"

"Well, there's a part of my brain that says if I don't count, something very bad will happen."

177, 178, 179, 180.

"Like what?"

Chelsea thought about describing some of the haunting images that rose unbidden from nowhere and clung to her consciousness like burrs: bloody worms with toothy mouths that burst from her stomach, razors slicing her eyes, flames engulfing her body and burning her skin black and red, the poison that would make her swell up and die, or the tractor trailer that would crush her chest as she biked home from work or school. . . .